Claudia and the Mystery at the Museum

The author gratefully acknowledges
Ellen Miles
for her help in
preparing this manuscript.

Claudia and the Mystery at the Museum

**Other books by
Ann M. Martin**

Rachel Parker, Kindergarten Show-off
Eleven Kids, One Summer
Ma and Pa Dracula
Yours Turly, Shirley
Ten Kids, No Pets
Slam Book
Just a Summer Romance
Missing Since Monday
With You and Without You
Me and Katie (the Pest)
Stage Fright
Inside Out
Bummer Summer

BABY-SITTERS LITTLE SISTER series
THE BABY-SITTERS CLUB mysteries
THE BABY-SITTERS CLUB series
(see back of the book for a more complete listing)

Claudia and the Mystery at the Museum
Ann M. Martin

AN
APPLE
PAPERBACK

SCHOLASTIC INC.
New York Toronto London Auckland Sydney

Cover art by Hodges Soileau

No part of this publication may be reproduced in whole or in part, or stored in a retrieval system, or transmitted in any form or by any means, electronic, mechanical, photocopying, recording, or otherwise, without written permission of the publisher. For information regarding permission, write to Scholastic Inc., 730 Broadway, New York, NY 10003.

ISBN 0-590-47049-3

12 11 10 9 8 7 6 5 4 3 2 1   3 4 5 6 7 8/9

Printed in the U.S.A.   28

First Scholastic printing, October 1993

"Claudia, what on earth are you *doing*?" asked my older sister Janine, when she saw me sprawled out on the living room floor, near the fireplace.

"Reading the paper," I said. "What does it *look* like I'm doing?" Janine is a genius (for real!), but sometimes she doesn't seem very bright at all.

"Not just the paper," said Janine. "You're reading *The New York Times*. The *Sunday New York Times*."

"I know that," I said, with dignity.

"But you *never* read the paper," said Janine. "Except perhaps to check your horoscope or something."

Janine was right, I had to admit it. I *don't* usually read our local newspaper, the *Stoneybrook News*, much less the Sunday *New York Times*. Normally, the tiny print and serious-looking columns of that huge, thick newspaper put me off. I'm not big on current events. Or history. Or politics.

But there was something in the *Times* that Sunday that I was really interested in reading about. So I was wading through page after page of dense black type, trying to find a certain article.

If you knew me the way my friends know me, you would be able to guess what that article was about. "Art," you'd say, without thinking twice.

And you'd be right. I may not be interested in geography or math or any of those other boring (to me) subjects, but I am very, very interested in art. I love to look at it. I love to read about it. And most of all, I like to make it. I like to draw and paint and sculpt. I like to make jewelry. I like to work with papier mâché. I'm never happier than when I'm creating something that's totally me.

"Totally me" means totally Claudia Kishi. And since I can't show you a piece of my artwork, I guess I'll just have to tell you about myself instead. I'm thirteen years old and I am in the eighth grade at Stoneybrook Middle School. That's in Stoneybrook, Connecticut, where I've lived all my life. It's a small quiet town with lots of nice old houses. As for my looks, I have long, straight black hair and dark almond-shaped eyes. In case you haven't

2

guessed, I am Asian (Japanese-American), and so are both of my parents.

My father is a partner in an investment firm in Stamford, which is the city nearest to our town. Don't ask me what he does, exactly, because I've never really understood it. It has something to do with money and numbers, that's all I know. My mother is the head librarian at the Stoneybrook Public Library. And my sister, as I told you before, is a genius.

Janine has always been smart. For example, she taught herself to read before she went to kindergarten. And now, even though she's only sixteen and a junior in high school, she takes classes at Stoneybrook University. Classes like physics and chemistry. And she gets all A's.

I get A's, too. But not in classes like English or social studies. I get A's in art. I'm not going to tell you my other grades, except to say that they're not so hot. It's not that I'm dumb. My teachers — and my parents — are always telling me that I have great "potential," and that if I "applied myself" I could do better in school. But I'd rather "apply myself" to a painting in progress, or to a new sculpture technique.

I mean, so what if I can't spell too well, or tell you what happened in the year 1016? Did Van Gogh know how to calculate what x equals? Probably not, and it sure didn't affect his painting. I've tried to get this point across to my parents, and I think they are beginning to understand. They are very supportive of my interest in art. Still, I know they wish I would do better in school.

They also wish I would a) stop eating junk food and b) stop reading Nancy Drew books. They don't like me to eat junk food because they say it's bad for me, but I have to say I haven't noticed any problems with my health. I can eat Chee tos and Milk Duds all day long, and I never gain weight or get pimples. I'm just lucky, I guess. As for the Nancy Drew books, my parents think I should be reading more "challenging" material. But I love mysteries, and that's all there is to it. So I hide my chips and candy and books all over my room, and I figure what my parents don't know won't hurt them.

Overall, I'd have to say that my family is pretty cool. Still, none of them understands me quite the way Mimi did. Mimi was my grandmother, and she lived with us until she died, which was not that long ago. She was always my favorite person. She had this *peace* around her, as if she just accepted the world and everyone in it. She always saw the best in people. I think of her every day, and I'll never stop missing her.

There's one other thing you should know about me, which is that I am a pretty wild dresser. I guess it's all part of my artistic nature. I love to put outrageous outfits together, and I *hate* looking like everyone else. I mean, I do wear trendy clothes, like leggings and big slouchy socks and Doc Marten boots, but I always add my own touches so that I stand out from the crowd. For instance, earrings I've made myself, or a big belt that I found in a thrift store. I also like to play around with my hair. One day I'll wear it in a French braid, and the next day it'll be in a ponytail on the top of my head.

That Sunday, my hair was in a long braid hanging down one side of my head, with red ribbons threaded into it. I was wearing a red-and-white striped shirt that hung down almost to my knees, red leggings, and black high-top sneakers. Even though I wasn't planning on going anywhere that afternoon, I had put some thought into my outfit. That's just the way I am.

I turned the pages of the Arts and Leisure section, hunting for the article I had heard about. My art teacher had mentioned it during class on Friday, and told us to look out for it.

"What are you looking for?" asked Janine, who had settled into the couch with the Book Review section.

5

"There's supposed to be an article in here about the new museum," I answered. "They're having a special show next week."

The new museum is one that recently opened in Stoneybrook. I've been really busy lately, so I haven't been there yet, but I've heard a lot about it. It isn't a huge museum, like the Metropolitan Museum in New York, but there's plenty to see, anyway. There are exhibits about science and history, and lots of special activities for kids. But a big part of the space is devoted to art. The museum doesn't have any Picassos yet, or anything like that, but they do have some work by lesser-known artists, which I was looking forward to seeing. Also, they plan on sponsoring special exhibits every so often — the kinds of exhibits I would never have had a chance to see before, unless I went to New York. There are a couple of small galleries in Stoneybrook, but nothing like this new museum.

I was pretty excited about it, but I got *really* excited when I finally found the article I'd been looking for in the *Times*. "Wow!" I said. "They're going to have a big show of Don Newman's stuff. A ret — retro — "

"A retrospective?" asked Janine. "That's when they show work that an artist has done over a long period of years."

"I knew that," I said. "I just couldn't pronounce the word right away. This is so amazing! I'll be able to see his early work."

"Who is Don Newman?" asked Janine.

"He's a sculptor," I answered. "A pretty famous one. And it just so happens that he lives near here, at least part of the year. That's why the Stoneybrook Museum gets to have the world premiere of this show."

"What kind of sculpture does he do?" asked Janine.

"Mostly abstract," I said. "I saw some of it in a museum in New York last year, and I loved it. He uses these big, rounded shapes, sort of like Henry Moore's stuff. But he's also influenced by Brancusi — these simple but radical forms. And some of his most recent stuff is a little bit like Noguchi's huge architectural style. But I hear his early work is really different. It looks more like Giacometti's long, thin human figures."

Janine stared at me. "You sound like an art critic," she said. "How do you *know* all that?" She looked very impressed.

I shrugged. "I don't know," I said. "I read about it, and look at books that have pictures of people's work." This didn't seem like a big deal to me, but I guess not everyone knows a Brancusi from a Noguchi. Anyway, I was kind of enjoying watching Janine's jaw drop. That's not a sight I see too often.

I went back to the article. "Oh, awesome," I said. "This piece I saw in New York is going to be there. It's called 'Daphne'."

"Daphne?" repeated Janine. "That's a name from the Roman myths. She was Apollo's first love, but she didn't love him back. In fact, she begged the gods to turn her into a tree so she could get away from him."

"That makes sense," I said, thoughtfully. "The sculpture is abstract, but when I saw it, I thought of a woman — *and* a tree. It's rounded, but there are these branches reaching up from it."

"Daphne became a laurel tree," said Janine, "and from then on laurel was very important to the Romans. They made laurel branches into wreaths, and . . ."

I had stopped listening. Janine has this habit of telling you more about certain subjects than you ever want to know. I've learned to tune her out. I had started thinking about something else, anyway. Here's what it was: I was dying to go to that show, and I wanted to take someone with me, to share it.

Right away I thought of some of the children I baby-sit for. I love to baby-sit. I do it a lot, and I'm even in a club that's about baby-sitting. It's called the BSC, for Baby-sitters Club, and my best friends are in it. I'll tell you more about it later. Anyway, I was giving art lessons to some of the kids around the time that Mimi died. And even though I was incredibly sad about losing Mimi, I was able to get a lot of pleasure out of teaching the kids to love art the way I do. I knew they would like the Newman show, and from what I had heard, there would be plenty of other things for them to see and do at the museum, too.

I headed for the phone. Janine was still droning on about Greek and Roman myths, but I ignored her. I made a few calls, and soon my plans were all set. I would go to the museum that Thursday, after school. And I would take three children with me: Corrie Addison, who had been one of my favorite art pupils, and the Arnold twins, Carolyn and Marilyn. I'm not sure who was looking forward to the trip more, me or the kids. Either way, I couldn't wait until Thursday.

CHAPTER 2

On Monday, Mom brought a book home from the library. It was about contemporary American artists, and it included a few pages about Don Newman. I read every word and studied the pictures. Then, on Tuesday, the *Stoneybrook News* carried a long article about the exhibit at the museum. I saw a picture of Don Newman, and he looked really neat — like a big teddy bear, with a full beard and horn-rimmed glasses.

As you can imagine, by Wednesday I was totally psyched for the show — and I still had to wait a day! That afternoon my friends came over to my house for a BSC meeting, and I think I almost drove them crazy raving about Don Newman's work.

"Enough, already, Claud," said Kristy. "It's time for the meeting to start, anyway." She pointed to my digital clock, which had just clicked to 5:30. Kristy Thomas is the president of the BSC, and she's very strict about meetings starting punctually.

Maybe the best way to tell you about my friends in the BSC is to tell you about this game we once played at a sleepover: If you had to be an animal, what kind of animal would you be?

Kristy said she would be a dog. That made sense — Kristy *loves* dogs. Her favorite hat has a picture of a collie on it, in memory of Louie, her first dog. Now her family has a Bernese Mountain dog puppy named Shannon. And Kristy is friendly and loyal and hardworking, so I guess she'd make a pretty good dog.

Kristy is the one who thought up the idea for the BSC. She realized how convenient it would be for parents to be able to dial one phone number and reach a whole bunch of experienced sitters, instead of having to make a zillion calls every time they needed someone to watch their kids. Like most of Kristy's ideas, this one was very simple, but it worked perfectly. The BSC has always had plenty of business. At first we advertised, with fliers and newspaper ads, but now we hardly ever need to do that. Satisfied parents are the only advertising we need.

Anyway, back to Kristy. She has long brown hair and brown eyes, and she's kind of short. She's not interested in fashion or makeup at all; she dresses in jeans and a turtleneck shirt just about every day. She says she's too busy to bother with dressing up, and I guess she is. She runs the BSC, coaches a softball team for little kids, and gets involved with all kinds of projects. Also, she has a huge family, so sometimes her house is chaotic. Kristy has two older brothers, Charlie and Sam, and one younger one, David Michael. That's the family she grew up with: her brothers and her mother. Her dad cut out on the family way back when David Michael was a baby.

But Kristy's family has changed — and grown — a lot in the last year or so. It all started when Kristy's mom fell in love with a man named Watson Brewer, who happens to be mega-rich. When they got married, Kristy and her brothers moved across town to live in Watson's mansion. (They used to live across the street from me.) Watson has two children from his first marriage, Karen and Andrew, who live with him part-time. And soon after their marriage, Watson and Kristy's mom decided to adopt a baby, so Emily Michelle came to live with them, too. She's an incredibly cute two-and-a-half-year-old Vietnamese girl. Soon after *she* arrived, Kristy's grandmother (everybody calls her Nannie) moved in to help out with everything. Full house, right? And that's not even counting the pets — Shannon, Boo-Boo the cat, and the goldfish.

I don't have any pets, but when the game got around to me, I decided I'd be a wildly colored jungle parrot. I envision plumes of red, gold, green, and blue. Purple tail feathers. A bright yellow beak. The flashiest, coolest bird in the jungle, that's me.

I'm vice-president of the club. I don't have many official duties, although I do make sure to have plenty of snacks on hand for meetings. The reason I'm vice-president is that I am the only one in the club with my own phone and a private line, so we don't tie up anyone else's phone with all the calls we get. That's important. We meet in my room three times a week, on Mondays, Wednesdays, and Fridays from five-thirty to six. That's a lot of phone time.

Our club treasurer is Stacey McGill, my best friend. The animal she picked was a big jungle cat, like a lion or a panther. I think that's perfect. Stacey has blonde hair, and huge eyes with dark, dark lashes, so she looks like one of those big, tawny cats. Plus, she has a certain elegance, as if she knows she's queen of the jungle.

Like me, Stacey likes clothes and fashion and experimenting with hairstyles and make-up. But while I'm a wild dresser, Stacey is more trendy and sophisticated. I think that's because she grew up in New York City. And she still visits there a lot, because her father lives there. Stacey's parents got divorced not that long ago, and Stacey (luckily for me!) decided to live in Stoneybrook with her mom.

Stacey may look like a queen, but she has down-to-earth problems, just like anybody else. The divorce was hard on her, for one thing. Also, she has diabetes, which is a disease that keeps your body from handling sugar the way it should. (No doubt Janine could give you the full scientific explanation, but I sure can't.) What that means for Stacey is that she has to keep track of every single thing she eats, and she has to be really careful about avoiding sweets. She can't eat Ring-Dings or candy bars, no matter how hungry she is. Also, she has to check her blood sugar all the time and give herself shots of this stuff called insulin, every day. It sounds gruesome, but Stacey makes it seem like no big deal. We all admire her for that.

As treasurer, Stacey keeps track of how much money we each earn. That's easy for her, since she's great at math. She also collects the club dues every Monday. We hate to pay up, but she makes us cough up the money. We use some of the treasury funds to pay

Kristy's brother to drive her to meetings. Some of the money goes for materials for our Kid-Kits, which are boxes full of games and books (mostly used) and stickers and crayons (those are new) that we sometimes bring with us on jobs. (Kid-Kits are another of Kristy's great ideas, by the way.) And once in a while we break into the treasury to splurge on a pizza party.

The club secretary is Mary Anne Spier. I'll tell you what she's like, and you can try to guess what animal she said she'd be. She's small, like Kristy (who happens to be her best friend), and she has brown hair and brown eyes. She recently got a great new haircut, and she looks terrific. She used to dress very conservatively, but that was only because her father insisted on it. He brought her up, since her mother died long ago, and he thought he had to be strict to be a good parent. He's finally loosened up a little, though, and now Mary Anne has some pretty cool clothes.

Mary Anne is very shy, but also very caring and sensitive. She has a romantic nature, which is probably why she's the only one of us who has a steady boyfriend. His name is Logan Bruno, and we all like him.

So, have you guessed? Mary Anne would like to be a koala. She said she would spend most of her time hiding in the trees, but she would also let herself be hugged by children, if they needed her.

Our koala makes a great secretary. Mary Anne is in charge of the club's record book, which includes information about our clients as well as the schedules of each sitter. At a glance, Mary Anne can tell you which of us is available for a job.

The club record book was Kristy's idea, of course, and so was the club notebook. The club notebook is where we write up jobs that we've been on, so that the other members can read our notes and keep up-to-date on what's happening with our clients — who's suddenly afraid of the dark, who's on a broccoli strike, and so on. All that writing and reading is a real pain sometimes, especially for a terrible speller like me, but I guess it pays off. Parents appreciate sitters who are well informed about their charges.

One member of the BSC wasn't in my room that afternoon, but I want to tell you about her anyway since she's still very much a part of the club. Her name is Dawn Schafer, and she's Mary Anne's *other* best friend — and her stepsister. Remember I mentioned that Mary Anne's father had loosened up a little? Well, we think it may have had something to do with the fact that he fell in love again with an old high school girlfriend, and then married her. That girlfriend was Dawn's mom, Sharon. She grew up in Stoneybrook, but after high school she moved to California. She got married there, and that's where Dawn and her younger brother Jeff were born. After the Schafers divorced, when Dawn was twelve, Sharon brought Dawn and Jeff back to Connecticut. Dawn adjusted to the move *pretty* easily, with the help of the BSC. But Jeff never got used to Connecticut, and he ended up moving back to California to live with his dad. Dawn missed him like crazy from the moment he left, so she finally decided to spend a few months with him and her dad, in California. She has promised to come back to Stoneybrook, though, and we all hope she makes it sooner rather than later. We miss her.

When Dawn had to choose an animal, she didn't hesitate. "A dolphin," she said. "I'd be perfectly happy skimming through the water and playing in the waves." I can see Dawn as a dolphin. She's certainly at home in the ocean, since she practically grew up on the beach.

Dawn was our alternate officer, which meant that she could take over for any other officer who had to miss a meeting. So far we haven't filled her job, and so far that's been okay. We've been attending meetings pretty regularly.

Now, so far all the members I've told you about are thirteen and in the eighth grade, like me. But two members of the BSC are younger. They are Jessi Ramsey and Mallory Pike. They're best friends, and they're eleven and in the sixth grade. They are junior officers, which means that they take mostly afternoon jobs, since they aren't allowed to sit at night except for their own families.

We didn't have to ask them which animal they'd choose. We knew they would both want to be horses. Jessi, who studies ballet seriously (and is very talented) said she'd be a Lipizzaner, which is a kind of stallion that is trained to dance in a special way. And Mallory, who loves to read and write (and wants to be an author someday), said she'd be a horse "just like Black Beauty in the book."

Jessi is African-American, with coal-dark eyes and long dancer's legs. She has a little sister named Becca and a baby brother named John Philip (everybody calls him Squirt). Her Aunt Cecelia lives with the family, too.

Mallory has red hair, freckles, glasses, and braces. She's going to be very, very pretty someday, but right now she can't see that. Mal comes from a gigantic family: she has seven brothers and sisters! She's the oldest, and then there're Adam, Byron, and Jordan (they're triplets), Vanessa, Nicky, Margo, and Claire. What a handful! I think they have been wearing Mal out lately. She's been feeling tired and run-down all the time.

Last but not least, the BSC has two associate members who don't always attend meetings. They help out when we're overbooked and need extra sitters. One of them is Logan Bruno, Mary Anne's boyfriend. He wasn't at our sleepover, of course, but Mary Anne told him about the game, and he said he'd be a hawk, so he could fly. The other is Shannon Kilbourne, who lives in Kristy's neighborhood. Lately Shannon's been coming to meetings more often so we're getting to know her better. She's really nice. I liked her animal choice. She said she would be a cat, so she could lie in front of a roaring fire all day.

So that's the zoo we call the BSC! Imagine if we'd actually turned into the animals we'd chosen. My room would have sounded like a jungle. But in reality the noises were pretty normal — girls talking and laughing, the phone ringing, and lots of crunching sounds as we passed around the popcorn I'd made for the meeting.

Just before the meeting broke up, Mal said she had some news. She told us that her mom was going to be very busy for awhile, putting in a lot of overtime with the temporary help agency she works for. She was going to be calling the BSC for plenty of sitters in the next few weeks. "Personally, I think she just wants to escape from the house," she said, laughing. "Claire is driving us all nuts. She saw *Annie* on TV last week, and now she's decided she wants to be a star. She's been bugging my parents to let her take tap or ballet or theater classes. And she walks around in sunglasses all the time and practices signing her autograph."

We all cracked up, picturing five-year-old Claire as a budding starlet. Then, as the meeting was ending, I brought up Don Newman again, *my* favorite local celebrity, but before long I noticed everybody seemed to be in a hurry to leave. I guess they just don't appreciate art the way I do.

CHAPTER 3

"**W**ow! Look at that!" Carolyn pulled on my left hand, guiding me toward a sign for an exhibit about the human body.

"No! Over here!" said Marilyn, pulling on my right hand. She was looking at an African mask that hung near a display of drums.

Corrie stood silently in the center of the main hall, gazing up at the large directory that told about the displays. Her eyes were sparkling as she read about the Discovery Room and the Science Room. "Can we see everything?" she asked, looking up at me.

"That's what we're here for," I answered. It was Thursday, and I had brought the three girls to the Stoneybrook Museum. I was as excited as they were, and not just because of the Don Newman exhibit. It turned out that the museum was a perfect place to bring kids. "Hold on," I said to the twins, who were still trying to pull me in opposite directions. "Let's take our time and look at everything."

The museum wasn't huge, or fancy, but the people who had built it had certainly packed a lot into it. In fact, I wasn't even sure we *could* see everything, not in one day. I knew I'd be coming back often, though. This museum was a special place.

It didn't *look* like your average museum. The floors were wood, instead of marble. There was no big echo-y hall, and there were no fancy paintings in gold frames. It was just a comfortable big building with white walls and lots of windows.

Corrie tugged on my sleeve. (I had dressed up a little, in pink lace leggings and a long black sweater. My hair was tied back with a pink ribbon, and I was wearing pink ballet-type flats.) "Can we go to the Discovery Room?" she asked. Corrie is a pretty, timid girl, with a serious face. She has brownish-blonde hair that's cut straight across her forehead in bangs, and long, dark eyelashes. She's small for her age, and something about her just makes me want to hug her.

"No!" cried Carolyn. "The Science Room! I want to shake hands with a skeleton." Carolyn loves science.

"I want to see the Music Center," said Marilyn. She plays the piano, and she's pretty good.

22

The twins look almost exactly alike. Marilyn has a tiny mole under her right eye, and Carolyn has one under her left eye. That's how I *used* to have to tell them apart. That was back when their mother used to dress them identically and treat them almost as one person. As they grew older, they became pretty tired of that, though, and now it's easy to tell them apart. Marilyn wears her brown hair long, and Carolyn wears hers short. Marilyn dresses simply, but Carolyn likes trendy clothes. And, as you might have noticed, they have very different interests.

I picked up a brochure with a museum map on it. "Let's start with the Discovery Room," I said. "It's upstairs. After that, we can check out the Science Room and the Music Center. Then we'll come back downstairs and see the sculptures. How does that sound?"

The girls nodded eagerly. The fact was that everything in the museum sounded interesting and fun, and we knew it didn't really matter *what* order we saw the exhibits in.

The Discovery Room was pretty cool. The first thing we saw when we walked in was a display on recycling, which included a giant robot the kids could hand soda cans to. There was a large supply of empty soda cans nearby. The robot would take the can and dump it into a box for recycling, and the kids were fascinated by watching the way it worked. I think they liked all the blinking lights on the robot.

The Discovery Room included an area devoted to teaching kids what it feels like to live with different disabilities. They could ride in wheelchairs, and try out crutches. A display showed how Braille works, with sample labels that the kids could "read" with their fingers. Also, there were mystery boxes. Kids had to try to guess their contents using only touch. Corrie loved that activity. "I think it's a bag of marbles," she said, grinning at me as she felt around in one of the boxes.

Carolyn and Marilyn were testing themselves at an electronic quiz board, which had buzzers that sounded and lights that lit up when they pushed a button for the right answer. "I'm a Whiz Kid," said Marilyn, pointing to the screen that showed her rating.

"And I'm a Junior Einstein," said Carolyn, proudly.

Even though we hadn't seen everything in the Discovery Room, we went on from there to the Science Room, by way of a "mole tunnel," which was so dark you had to feel your way through. When we came out into the light, blinking like overgrown moles, Carolyn ran straight to a human skeleton that stood in the corner. "Nice to meet you, Mr. Bones," she said, shaking its hand.

Marilyn and Corrie refused to go near it. "Too scary," said Marilyn. Corrie nodded in agreement. They headed for the collection of fossils, shark jaws, dinosaur bones, and birds' nests, which were laid out so that kids could pick them up and hold them. "Please Touch," said a big sign. I thought that was so cool. How many museums have you seen with a sign like that? Usually the exhibits are behind glass, or ropes, and you feel as if the guards will drag you off to jail if you even dare to breathe on anything.

"Claudia, look at me!" Carolyn had left the skeleton and was standing near a big, round metal globe. She put her hand on it, and suddenly her hair was standing on end.

"Carolyn!" I cried. "Are you all right?" I ran to her.

"I'm fine," she said, giggling. "It doesn't hurt or anything. It's a machine that makes static electricity. It's called a Van de Graaff generator, and — "

"It's awesome," I said, cutting her off. I could tell that she was about to pull a "Janine" on me, and tell me more than I wanted to know about Van de Graaff generators. I reached out my hand, touched it gingerly, and felt the strangest sensation — my hair standing on end. But Carolyn was right. It didn't hurt.

"Can we go to the Music Center now?" asked Marilyn.

"But we haven't seen everything yet," said Carolyn. "What about the shadow wall, and the climb-in kaleidoscope? What about the video phone?"

"We'll come back soon," I said as I herded the girls down the hall. I was beginning to realize how much there was to see at the museum, and I knew we wouldn't reach the Newman exhibit if we didn't move along. I was determined to see it that afternoon.

The Music Center quickly became Marilyn's favorite place. It included a player piano, an electric organ, and lots of smaller instruments, including wind chimes and xylophones. In one corner a microphone stood on a platform. Kids could talk or sing into it, and a video screen showed what the sound waves you were creating looked like. The girls ran from exhibit to exhibit, trying to take everything in.

I almost felt bad about pulling them away, but I was sure they'd like Don Newman's sculptures, too. And suddenly I couldn't wait another minute. I *had* to see "Daphne."

"Let's go, you guys," I said. "The museum closes pretty soon, and I wanted to show you something special today." We headed downstairs, to the art rooms. I asked a guard which way to go. He pointed me toward a yellow hallway and told me to follow a group of people headed down it.

I led the girls down the hall. They were talking excitedly about everything they had seen upstairs.

Suddenly, a piercing electronic shriek interrupted them. "Oh, my lord!" I said.

"What *is* that?" cried Marilyn, over the sound.

"I think it's a fire alarm," I said. "Come on!" I hurried the girls toward the EXIT sign I saw ahead.

Just as we reached the door, the noise stopped. And then I heard another sound: breaking glass! After that, I heard a *different* type of alarm. This one was more like the bell between classes at my school, only ten times louder.

"What's *that*?" asked Carolyn.

"It must be a burglar alarm," I said as I watched two security guards rush past us. They ran into a nearby room, which was where the sound of breaking glass had come from. I had no idea what was going on, but I wasn't about to take the time to find out. The most important thing was to get the girls out of the building. You don't mess around when you hear a fire alarm.

I pushed open the door, and we stepped into a little courtyard that was already full of frightened-looking people. Nobody seemed to know what was happening. "I think we better go home," I said to the girls, "and come back another day."

They were clustered around me, and all three of them looked scared. "I want my mommy," said Corrie.

I knew how she felt. I kind of wanted *my* mommy, too! But instead of my mom, a guard showed up. "We'll have to ask you folks not to leave. Please stay in the area," he said. "There's been a burglary. Some extremely valuable ancient coins have been stolen, and each of you will have to be searched before you can leave."

The girls gasped. So did I. I heard a lot of people around me gasp, too. A whole Brownie troop was standing nearby, their two leaders looking nervous. I also noticed a custodian with his mop and pail, and a nicely dressed man who had one blue eye and one green eye. My Nancy Drew books have taught me to notice things like that — especially when a crime has taken place. It's important to pay attention to all the possible suspects. I looked around and checked out everybody else in the courtyard as the guard began escorting us back into the museum, but nobody looked especially suspicious.

As the guard led us down the hall, I noticed

that he was passing the room where I'd heard glass breaking. I hung back and peered inside it as I walked slowly by. There, in plain sight, was a big display case that had once had a glass front. Now the glass was in shards all over the inside of the case, and the case was empty. Someone must have tripped the fire alarm as a distraction, smashed the front of the case, grabbed a handful of coins, and run off. I could almost picture it happening.

"Come along, miss," said the guard, ushering the girls and me into a small room, where a female guard was waiting.

"Don't worry," she said to us. "This won't take long." She searched us quickly, smiling as if she knew we couldn't possibly be the criminals.

As we left the museum, the girls talked about what had happened. I was silent. I was trying to remember every detail, so I could think about the incident later on. I cared about the museum, and I hated the idea that somebody had robbed it. I wanted to help solve this mystery, whatever it took.

CHAPTER 4

I opened my closet door and threw in an arm-load of clothes and shoes. Then I shoved a pile of books under the bed. I pushed a stack of art supplies (construction paper and pastel crayons) to the side of my desk, smoothed out the bedspread over my unmade bed, and tucked a batch of makeup behind my dressing-table mirror. Finally, I stood in the center of my room, with my hands on my hips. It looked better than it had three minutes before, when I'd realized it needed a little tidying. Nobody would ever mistake me for a "clean freak," but once in a while even I'm embarrassed by how messy my room can be. My friends would be arriving any minute for a BSC meeting, and for once I wanted my room to look presentable.

Kristy was, as usual, the first to arrive. I waited for her to comment on how neat my room looked, but she didn't seem to notice.

Neither did Stacey, when she came in, nor Mary Anne. Jessi and Mal weren't impressed either. They just walked in and took their usual places on the floor near the bed. Shannon was the last to arrive, and I was *sure* she would say something. But she didn't. Instead, she just accepted the bag of Doritos I passed to her, fished out a handful, and passed the bag on to Mary Anne.

I guess the reason that nobody commented on my room was that they were too excited about the robbery at the museum. I had called them the night before and told them a little about what had happened, but they were dying to hear the details.

I was disappointed that my friends hadn't noticed my clean room, but I forgot about that when we started to talk about the robbery. As soon as she had called the meeting to order, Kristy held up the afternoon edition of the *Stoneybrook News*. "Did you guys see this?" she asked. "There's a whole big article about what happened yesterday."

My friends and I clustered around her and read over her shoulder. "New Museum Robbed" said the headline. We saw a picture of the outside of the museum, with police cars parked in front of it. "Police are investigating yesterday's robbery of precious coins from the Stoneybrook Museum," said the article. It went on to say that the coins were "irreplace-able," and that there were, so far, no solid clues as to their whereabouts. There were quotes from the museum curator and from outraged citizens. Everyone was shocked that the museum had been robbed — and so soon after its grand opening.

"I can't believe you were right there when it happened," Kristy said to me. "Tell us everything you saw and heard. Were you any-where near the room where the coins were?"

"We were just down the hall from it," I said, remembering how I'd heard the sound of breaking glass. I told my friends about the robbery. "It was pretty exciting," I said. "First of all, I thought there was a fire somewhere because the fire alarm went off. That was scary, since I was responsible for the girls. Then, on top of that, *another* alarm went off, and the guards herded us all back into the museum to be searched."

"Wow, just like on TV!" said Stacey. "Did you see anyone suspicious?"

"I don't know," I said, honestly. "There was this guy with one blue eye and one green eye, and a whole troop of Brownies. The custodian was there, with his mop and pail. But nobody looked really suspicious. I mean, there weren't any guys with trenchcoats and briefcases or anything." I paused to munch on a Dorito.

"I wonder where those coins are now," said Shannon. Her eyes were gleaming. She likes a mystery as much as the rest of us. "I mean, they could be anywhere."

"Not really," said Mal. She had been listening closely to everything I had said, and I had noticed her reading the article very carefully. "Those coins are still somewhere inside the museum."

"What?" exclaimed Stacey. "How can you be sure?"

Mallory held up her hand and started ticking off points on her fingers. "First of all, when the alarm sounded, they made sure all the exits were guarded. Nobody was allowed to leave. Then they searched everybody who had been inside — *including* the guards and the staff. There's almost no way the coins could have left the building."

"Wow," I said softly. "You're right. I didn't think of that."

Kristy leaned forward. "So where do you think they are?" she asked Mal.

Mal put down her hand and shrugged. "I have no idea," she said. "All I know is that they must be in the museum."

The phone began to ring then, and for the next few minutes we were busy setting up jobs. Or, at least, everyone else was busy. I was just sitting there, thinking as hard as I could. As soon as Kristy finished with the last call, I spoke up. "Okay," I said. "I've thought of a few places where the coins might be."

"So have I," said Jessi. Obviously, she had been thinking, too. "But you go first, Claud."

"They could have been dropped into the donation box," I said. "It's a big steel case near the front entrance. You're supposed to donate some money every time you come to the museum. You don't *have* to — it's not like paying admission — but if you can, you should."

"Did *you* donate?" asked Stacey playfully. She must have thought I was getting a little too serious about things.

"Of course!" I said. "The girls each put in a quarter, and I put in two dollars." I took another handful of Doritos. "Okay, next possible place. How about the museum gift shop? We took a quick look at it yesterday, and I noticed that they sell reproductions of the ancient coins. The thief could have put the *real* coins in with the fake ones, and nobody would know the difference." I stopped and looked around. I was proud of my ideas, and I could see that everyone else thought they were good, too. Mary Anne was taking notes. Kristy was nodding and biting on the pencil she usually keeps behind her ear. "What about your ideas, Jessi?" I asked.

"I really only have one," she said. "I heard that the museum has a big fountain in the courtyard. And you know how people throw pennies into fountains, to make wishes? Maybe the thief threw the coins in there, hoping nobody would notice them."

"Great," said Mary Anne, making a note of Jessi's idea.

"I guess we've already decided that we're going to try to solve this mystery," said Kristy, raising her eyebrows.

"Definitely," I said. "I mean, sure the police are working on it. But I was *there* when it happened. There's no way I can forget about it now. Plus, that museum is really important to me. It just opened, and I'd hate to see it close because of this."

"Okay," said Kristy. "So what do we do next?"

"Well," I said, "I guess we go back to the museum and check out some of these ideas. Maybe we'll come up with some others, too. Plus, we have to watch out for suspicious characters."

"Like the man with one green eye and one blue eye?" asked Shannon.

"Sure," I said. "Anybody who was there is a suspect." I thought for a second. "Except me, of course. And except for Corrie and Carolyn and Marilyn."

"Even the Brownies?" asked Stacey, with a twinkle in her eye.

"Even the Brownies," I answered solemnly. "Who knows? They could have stashed the coins under one of their beanies or something." I giggled.

Everybody else cracked up, too. "Gotta watch out for those Brownies," said Kristy.

Mal had picked up the newspaper again. "It says here that all kinds of events are coming up at the museum," she said. "They're really trying to make the first month exciting, to give the museum a push. It will take a lot of community support to keep the museum going."

I nodded. "My parents have been saying the same thing," I said. "So what's going on there?"

"Well, there's a big formal party planned for the last night of the Don Newman exhibit. Plus a cocktail party to celebrate the museum's one month anniversary. And they're going to have a special exhibit about historical Stoneybrook."

"Those would be perfect opportunities for us to do a lot of detective work," said Kristy.

"Wouldn't it be cool if we could somehow go to the Don Newman party?" I said dreamily. "I'd give anything to meet him."

"Yeah, but there's no way any of us could get invited to that," said Mal. "It's going to be really fancy. Black tie, it says here. That means it's formal. I bet the only people who get invited are the rich ones who gave the museum a lot of money."

We all looked at Kristy then. Her stepfather is the only really rich person we know. She shook her head. "I don't think Watson gave money to the museum," she said.

"Oh, well," I said. "Even if we can't go to the parties, we can check out the historical thing, and we can still walk into the museum anytime we want. Who wants to go there with me tomorrow?" I looked around the room. It was obvious that *everyone* wanted to. "Great," I said. "Why don't we meet here at about — " Just then, the phone rang again. Kristy picked it up.

"Sure, Mrs. Pike," she said, raising her eyebrows at Mal. "No problem. We'll have someone there." She hung up. "Your mom says she and your dad are taking your brothers and sisters to the mall tomorrow to shop for school clothes. She wants you to go along, and since you haven't been feeling well, she was hoping another sitter could go, too."

Mal rolled her eyes and flopped down on the floor. "Good-bye, museum," she said, good-humoredly. "When you have a big family, clothes-shopping is like an Olympic event. I'm exhausted just thinking about it. But there's no way I can get out of this."

"I'll go with you," volunteered Mary Anne. As usual, she was being sweet and sensitive. "I saw a sweater I wanted last time I was there."

The rest of us made plans to meet at the museum the next morning.

"Okay," said Kristy, a few minutes later, "meeting adjourned. Oh, and by the way, Claudia," she added. "Good job cleaning your room." She nodded toward my closet door, which had fallen open. A huge pile of clothes was cascading out of it. I blushed as everybody cracked up. Then I started laughing, too. At least they had noticed I *tried*.

CHAPTER 5

Saturday

Mal, maybe your parents should look into shopping through catalogs! I mean, taking seven kids to the mall to shop for school clothes is an awesome task. On the other hand, even though we baby-sitters and the adults were totally exhausted by the end of the day, the kids did have a lot of fun — especially Claire. Plus, everyone got new clothes. So, the trip was worthwhile.

Mary Anne arrived at the Pike house that morning just as Mr. and Mrs. Pike were starting to load the kids into the two cars they would be taking to the mall. (Whenever the Pikes take a family trip, they have to take two cars. Someday maybe they'll be able to buy one of those mini-vans, but until then, they use this system.) Getting the kids set to go somewhere can take awhile. Mrs. Pike once said that it's like trying to herd sheep into a pen, and that maybe a good sheepdog would come in handy.

"Byron," she called. "Adam, Jordan! Put down those swords and get into the car!" The triplets, who are ten years old, have been playing "knight" lately. Basically, that means they spend a lot of time bashing each other with these silly-looking foam rubber swords.

"Take that, you varlet!" said Adam, landing one last blow on Jordan's shoulder. He dashed into the car before Jordan could hit him back, and his brothers chased after him. Mrs. Pike closed the back door of the station wagon as soon as the three of them had jumped in.

"Three down, four to go," she said. "Claire! Margo! Time to get in the car."

Claire, who's five, was performing a tap dance on the concrete floor of the garage. She had bribed seven-year-old Margo to be her audience by promising to give her her share of dessert that night. "On the goooooood ship, Lollipop," she sang, as she tapped away. Margo pretended to watch politely, but Mary Anne could see that she had a book hidden in her lap. She turned a page every time Claire turned her back. When Margo heard her mother calling, she looked relieved. "Coming," she said, dragging a still-singing Claire along with her.

"Where's Nicky?" asked Mrs. Pike, when Mr. Pike came outside to see how the loading process was going.

"He's upstairs, changing his socks," said Adam, before Mr. Pike had a chance to answer. "He's been wearing the same ones for, like, three weeks, and Mal told him he had to put on fresh ones if he was going to try on new shoes today." Nicky is eight, and he doesn't believe in "wasting" clean clothes by changing too often.

Mrs. Pike nodded approvingly. "And Vanessa?"

"She's up in her room, putting the finishing touches on a poem," answered Mr. Pike. "She says she'll be right down." Vanessa, who's nine, wants to be a poet when she grows up. She likes to compose poems for special occasions, and she likes to share them, so whoever rode in the car with her would probably be

41

treated to a recitation of "An Ode to the Mall," or something like that.

By the time Nicky and Vanessa ran downstairs, Claire had decided she needed to use the bathroom one last time. When Claire climbed into the car, Margo realized she had forgotten to bring her "barf bag," which she usually needs on long car rides, so she ran back into the house. Then Adam remembered some hidden money he'd saved from his last allowance, and he dashed to his room to find it.

Finally, all seven kids, plus Mal and Mary Anne, plus Mr. and Mrs. Pike, were packed into the two cars. They pulled out of the driveway and started down the street, with Claire singing, "We're off to see the ma-all, the wonderful Washington Mall," to the tune of "We're Off To See the Wizard."

The trip to the mall was uneventful. Mary Anne told me later that she had been riding next to Margo, and had worried about Margo "hurling," as the triplets put it, but although Margo *had* looked a little pale for a few minutes, the barf bag turned out to be unnecessary. "Lucky me," said Mary Anne, with relief.

As soon as the cars were parked, the trip went into high gear. Everyone piled out and ran into the mall, ignoring Mr. and Mrs. Pike's pleas to stay together and "proceed in an organized fashion." The triplets and Nicky headed straight for the video arcade, and Mal and her dad had to run after them and drag them to the shoe store. Claire and Margo let their noses lead them to the store that sells giant chocolate chip cookies, and they stood there with their faces pressed against the window until Mrs. Pike convinced them to follow her to the department store where they were going to look for clothes. Vanessa wandered dreamily around the fountain that splashes in the middle of the mall, watching the poetic way the water rose and fell. Mary Anne had to listen to Vanessa's "Fountain" haiku before she could convince her to join the other girls in looking over new sweaters and blouses. Seeing the fountain reminded Mary Anne of the fountain we were going to check at the museum, but she had no time to stop and think about the mystery.

After the "first round," as Mrs. Pike called the first hour or so of shopping, everyone gathered for lunch at the pizza parlor. Mrs. Pike pulled a long list from her shoulder bag and began to check off items that had already been bought. "Nicky — sneakers," she said, making a check mark. "Vanessa — white blouse. Claire — sweater and skirt. Adam, Jordan, and Byron — good shoes." She sighed. "We still have a long way to go," she reported. "The girls all need shoes, and the boys *have* to have some new jeans. Shirts, too."

"I saw a pair of boots I liked when I was with Dad and the boys at the shoe store," said Mal. "I'll go back there with you and the girls."

"And I still want to check out that sweater I saw," said Mary Anne. "I'll go back to the department store and help the boys find what they need."

"You two are great," said Mr. Pike to Mal and Mary Anne. "There's no way we could do this without you." He took a handkerchief out of his pocket and wiped his forehead. He looked very tired. Helping four boys try on shoes had not been easy.

Claire shrieked. "Nicky, stop it!" she cried. "Mommy, Nicky chewed his pizza and then opened his mouth and showed it to me."

"Ew," said Mary Anne. She felt a little sick just *thinking* about how chewed pizza would look.

"Did not!" said Nicky, swallowing quickly.

"Did too!" said Claire.

"That's enough," said Mrs. Pike. "Nicky, if you want to play 'see-food,' play it with your brothers. The rest of us aren't interested." Mary Anne admired Mrs. Pike's matter-of-fact tone, and realized she must have been through this argument a thousand times before. You can always learn something new about dealing with kids from watching Mr. and Mrs. Pike deal with theirs.

"Ready?" asked Mr. Pike.

"Just about," said Mrs. Pike, taking a last sip of water.

"Mom, can I have another piece of pizza?" asked Adam. "I dropped mine on the floor."

"Did you?" she asked, raising her eyebrows. "I could have sworn I saw you eat it. And there aren't any slices on the floor."

"Well," said Adam. "A dog came and ate it?"

"Let's go," said Mr. Pike, ignoring the situation. "I want to get home sometime before midnight."

The Pikes and Mary Anne headed out of the pizza place and down a corridor they hadn't yet explored. Claire ran ahead to check out a display in the center of the hall. Then she ran back. Her cheeks were pink, and her eyes were gleaming. "Mommy!" she said. "Daddy! There's something I have to show you." She grabbed their hands and pulled them toward the display. "Look," she said. "I can make a really professional movie here! It's just what I always wanted to do. Can I? Please? Pretty please?"

Mr. and Mrs. Pike looked the booth over. So did Mary Anne, Mal, and the rest of the kids. They saw that customers could be videotaped as if they were playing a part in a movie. They could dress in a costume, stand in front of a backdrop, and sing along to a pre-recorded tape.

Mary Anne saw an orphanage set for *Annie*, along with a curly haired wig and a red dress. She saw a set of the Ghostbusters' office, and official-looking Ghostbuster outfits. And she saw —

"The yellow brick road!" cried Claire. "I can wear that blue dress and look just like Dorothy!" She turned to her parents again. "Oh, Mommy, *please*? I promise I'll be good for the rest of my life."

Mrs. Pike turned to Mr. Pike and raised her eyebrows. He shook his head slightly, pointing to the price on the sign. She looked at it and winced. "Are you sure you want to do this, Claire?" she asked. "It's very expensive."

"I want to do it more than anything in the whole wide world," said Claire passionately.

Finally, Mr. and Mrs. Pike relented. "All right, honey," said Mrs. Pike. "I guess we can count this as an early Christmas present. Now, where do we go?" She glanced behind the booth and gasped. "My goodness, there's a long line," she said.

"No way I'm waiting in line," said Nicky. "I have important stuff to do."

"We all do," said Mr. Pike. "Claire, we can come back another day," he began, but Claire started to wail.

"Why don't I wait with her?" asked Mary Anne. "I don't mind, really." She was just as glad to avoid jeans-shopping with the boys. And that's how Mary Anne ended up watching Claire make her film debut.

"She was really very good," Mary Anne told me later. Claire spent her time waiting in line figuring out what to sing, and finally decided on "Somewhere Over the Rainbow," even though, as she pointed out, Dorothy really sings that song in Kansas and not when she's on the Yellow Brick Road in Oz. When she reached the head of the line, she put on the blue gingham dress, slipped the prop picnic basket over her arm, stepped onto the set, and sang her heart out. "The other people on line actually applauded," said Mary Anne, when she finished telling me the story.

And Claire hugged her "professional video" to her chest all the way home from the mall, looking happier and prouder than an actor with an Oscar.

CHAPTER 6

"Awesome!" said Kristy, looking around the Discovery Room. "Karen and Andrew and David Michael are going to *love* this."

"So will Becca," said Jessi. "We'll have to bring *all* the kids we sit for. This'll be great for rainy days."

"Wait till Charlotte gets a look at that robot," said Stacey. She was talking about Charlotte Johanssen, who is one of her favorite kids to sit for.

Shannon was looking at the exhibit about physical disabilities. "It really makes you understand how hard this could be," she said. She sat in a wheelchair and wheeled herself around for a minute. "Whew!" she said. "That takes a lot of muscle power."

My friends and I were back at the museum (in case you haven't guessed), and they seemed just as excited about it as I had been. They wanted to see *everything*. I led them through the mole tunnel and into the Science Room, where Kristy insisted on shaking hands with the skeleton and Shannon tried out the Van de Graaff generator. We all cracked up when her long, thick hair stood on end.

"I think you should wear your hair that way the next time you go to a dance," I said. "It looks super-chilly." (That's what my friends and I say when we mean "cool.")

We toured the Music Room next. Each of us picked up an instrument and started playing it, and soon the room was full of sound. I wouldn't exactly call it *music*. It sounded like some kind of insane orchestra — without a conductor. The noise made us laugh so hard we could hardly stop.

"Okay," said Kristy, when we had caught our breath. "Time to get down to work." She turned to me. "First of all, where's the room the coins were stolen from? Let's take a look at that."

I led my friends downstairs, hardly glancing at the displays of coins from other countries or the diorama showing how coins are made. I led them straight to the case that had been broken into. The glass had been fixed, but the case was empty. A sign on the case said, "This display is temporarily closed. We apologize for the inconvenience." My friends and I examined the case from all angles.

Suddenly a man in a uniform stepped into our circle. "Can I help you with something?" he asked.

"Uh, no," I said. "We were just curious about the robbery."

"The police are taking care of it," said the guard. "Meanwhile, the museum is under heavy security. A twenty-four-hour guard has been posted in every room."

He sounded as if he were warning us not to snoop around too much. I felt like telling him what good detectives we could be. I probably cared about the museum ten times more than the police did. But I knew I should keep those thoughts to myself. "That's good," I said. "You can't be too careful." My friends and I backed out of the room.

"Boy, we better watch out," said Stacey. "We don't want them to think *we're* the robbers. I mean, if they see us hanging around acting nosy, they might get suspicious."

"No way," argued Kristy. "A bunch of teenage girls?"

"Well, anyway," I said. "We have other stuff to do before we leave today. Like check out the gift shop."

"And the fountain," added Jessi.

"Right," said Shannon. "I just wish we could find a way to check out that donation box."

"We'll never be able to do that without looking suspicious," I said. "But maybe, if we ask the right questions . . ." I was getting an idea. "Come on," I said. I headed for the main lobby. A woman was at the information booth. "Excuse me," I said. "We're, uh, doing a class project on Stoneybrook's feelings about the new museum. I was just wondering if you could tell me how much money you're taking in with that donation box." I pointed to the steel box.

"People have been very generous," said the woman. "Let's see." She checked a notebook that lay on her desk. "As of last night, we've taken in over six hundred dollars this week."

"That's great," I said. "So, you empty the box every night to count the money?"

She gave me a funny look. "Yes, we do," she said. "With an armed guard present, of course."

"Naturally," I said. "Thanks so much for your time." I scurried off, my friends close behind me. When we were far enough away, Kristy gave me a high five.

"Great job, Claud," she said. "That's all we needed to know. If they empty the box every night, the thief couldn't have put the coins in there. They'd have been discovered right away."

"Whew," I said. "That was a little risky, but

it was worth it. Ready to check out the gift shop?"

"Do we have a plan?" asked Jessi.

I shook my head. "No, but we'll think of something. Come on!"

When we reached the gift shop, we spread out and started browsing, trying to look casual. Stacey and I checked out the postcards. Kristy was looking at the toys, mostly educational games and models based on exhibits in the Discovery and Science rooms. Jessi looked over the calendars, and Shannon examined some fossils.

Then, one by one, we drifted past the case where the coins were kept.

"Gee, those look almost real," I heard Jessi say innocently, to the man behind the counter.

He nodded, bored. He was reading a magazine as he sat waiting for customers.

"These must look exactly like the ones that were stolen," Shannon said.

"Just about," said the man, yawning and turning a page in his magazine.

"But they're copies, right?" asked Stacey.

"Uh-huh," said the man.

"Really *good* copies," said Kristy. "I mean, how could you ever tell the difference?"

Good question, I thought. Now he would have to explain how to tell the real ones from the fakes.

"Oh, we have our ways," he said.

Darn!

But then he put down his magazine and went on. "For one thing, the fakes are really just foil-covered chocolate coins," he said. He unlocked the case and pulled one out. "See?" He showed it to us. We were all clustered around the case by that time.

"Awesome," said Kristy. "They look so real."

"Not once you know the difference," the man said, sounding bored again.

We leaned over the case, trying not to fog it with our breathing, and looked closely at each of the coins. Sure enough, every one had a little seam around the edge, where the two pieces of foil came together. We looked at each other, shrugged, and left the gift shop.

"Well, that's another theory down the drain," said Kristy. "One more place to check. Who feels like taking a dip?"

"You mean, in the fountain?" Jessi squealed. "We can't jump into it! Somebody would notice."

"Just kidding," said Kristy. "It didn't look that deep when we went past it before. We can lean over the edge and feel around for coins."

And that's what we did. We took turns. One of us watched for the guard, who walked by every few minutes. The others, trying to act natural so as not to draw attention, leaned over and fished around in the water. Fifteen minutes later, we were all soaked up to our elbows, and Shannon's purse was damp from being splashed with water. We had found all kinds of coins: pennies, nickels, dimes, and quarters, plus one Canadian penny and a subway token from New York City. But no ancient coins were to be found. We threw the money back in the fountain. "I'm going to make a wish," said Jessi. "Even though these have been wished on once already, they might work again."

We all wished. And we probably all wished for the same thing: that we would be able to solve the case of the stolen coins. I know that's what *I* wished for, anyway.

We sat on the edge of the fountain, trying to figure out what to do next. "I guess we're out of places to search for the coins," I said. "I hate to give up, but as long as we're here, does anybody want to see the Don Newman exhibit? I haven't seen it yet, and I'm dying to."

"Why not?" asked Kristy. "Lead us to it."

I started off down a hall, eager to see the exhibit. But suddenly Jessi tugged on my arm. "Claud!" she said. "Did you see that man's eyes?" I shook my head. I had barely noticed the man who had just passed us in the hall. "One was blue, and the other was green!" she said. We all turned in our tracks and hurried to catch up with the man.

He headed upstairs and into the Music Room. "That's him!" I hissed, as I watched him pick up a tambourine. "He's not dressed the same, but it's definitely him. What's he doing here again?"

"Maybe he just didn't get a good look at the exhibits before," said Kristy. "The robbery interrupted his visit, so he came back. Just like you."

"Maybe," I said. But the man didn't seem to be paying much attention to the exhibits. He wandered from instrument to instrument, and then he left the room. "Let's tail him," I said. "Something about him doesn't seem right."

We followed that man all over the museum. After the Music Room, he checked out the Discovery Room. Again, he just seemed to be wandering around. He barely noticed the electronic quiz board, even though its lights were flashing like crazy. Then we followed him through the mole tunnel and into the Science Room. I saw him bump into the skeleton by mistake, and heard him say, "Oh! Excuse me," before he realized it wasn't a person. I put my hand over my mouth to stifle my giggles, but he heard me anyway. He flashed me an irritated look.

I wished he would go to the Don Newman exhibit, just so I would get a chance to see it, but he didn't. He *did* go downstairs, but instead of heading for the sculptures he wandered into the room where the coins had been displayed and examined the empty case as if he found it fascinating. While we were in the room with him, Kristy stumbled into a display case and almost fell. "Whoops!" she said. The man glared at her.

Finally, we shadowed the man right out into the parking lot and watched as he climbed into his car. I think he knew we were following him, because he kept turning to glance at us. Each time, he looked more annoyed.

We watched him drive off. "Think he's the robber?" Kristy asked.

"I don't know," I said. "But there's definitely something weird about him, don't you think?" Everyone agreed. But none of us could imagine any way to prove he had stolen the coins. Our investigation had come to a dead end.

CHAPTER 7

My friends and I sat on the steps of the museum, feeling glum. We had been so excited about working on the case of the missing coins, but so far all our leads had petered out. We didn't know what else we could do, for the time being.

Kristy checked her watch. "I better get home," she said. "I told my mom I would help watch the kids this afternoon."

Shannon and Jessi said they had to leave, too.

"Well, I'm going to stay and check out the Don Newman exhibit," I said. "That was my original reason for coming to the museum, and I still haven't even gotten *near* it."

"I'll come with you," said Stacey. "You've talked about these sculptures so much that I'm curious about them. Besides, I don't have any other plans."

I smiled at her. Stacey's not really interested in art, and I knew she was just staying with me to be friendly. "You might be surprised," I said. "I bet you'll like this stuff."

We said good-bye to the others and headed back into the museum. As we approached the big glass doors of the main entrance, I caught a glimpse of our reflections. We looked as well-dressed and sophisticated as any big-city museum-goers. I smiled at Stacey as I opened the door and ushered her in. "After you, my dear," I said.

"Oh, no, no, no!" she said, smiling back. "After you!" We giggled as we squeezed through together.

I led Stacey toward the gallery where Don Newman's work was being shown. "His stuff isn't very realistic," I warned her. "I mean, a sculpture might not *look* like a person, or a certain animal or anything. He just *suggests* things by the way he uses form and line."

"Gotcha," she said. "I'll just follow you around and you can tell me about what we're looking at."

By that time we had arrived at the entrance to the gallery. I went in, with Stacey behind me. "Wow!" I said. "Nice space." In case you don't know, "space" is very important when you're showing artwork. It has to be open and bright and welcoming, and this room was all of those things. I began to fantasize about showing my *own* artwork there. Suppose, just suppose, I was introduced to the curator of the museum. "Did you say your name was Claudia *Kishi*?" he would ask, looking surprised. "I've heard about you. The word is that you are the most talented and promising student in the Stoneybrook schools. Could you — *would* you — consider showing in our modest gallery?"

"I'd be delighted to," I would say. "I feel it's important to give something *back* to the community you're from. Why don't you call me to schedule a possible time? I'm sure I can fit you in between my upcoming shows at the Museum of Modern Art and the Guggenheim."

"Claudia!" Stacey was tugging on my arm. "Why are you grinning like that?"

I came out of my daydream. "Oh, I guess I'm just happy to be here," I said lamely. "Look!" I continued, changing the subject. "This is a wonderful piece." We walked over to a grouping of three sculptures, two larger ones and one smaller one. They seemed to be in a kind of embrace.

"It's like a family," said Stacey. "Mother, father, and child."

"You're right," I said, reaching out to stroke the "child's" back.

"Claud!" cried Stacey. "What are you doing? You can't touch that!" She glanced nervously at the guard who stood nearby.

"It's okay," I reassured her. "Look at the sign." I pointed to the wall near the gallery door. On it was a sign like the one in the Discovery Room. "Please Touch," it said. "Don Newman believes that art should be touchable," I told Stacey. I smiled at her, and noticed that the guard was smiling, too. "He thinks art should involve more senses than just sight," I went on. "When I saw his pieces in New York, the same sign was up, and everyone in the gallery was touching the sculptures."

I walked over to another piece, and went on talking. "He even builds in special features that you wouldn't know about *unless* you touched the pieces," I said, "See how this one moves when I push it a little?" We were standing near a sculpture that looked like an old boulder that had been lying in a riverbed for hundreds of years. It was rounded and worn, and kind of — well, kind of friendly. That may sound weird, but it's really the only way to describe it. I touched it, and it shifted its weight just a little.

"Awesome," said Stacey, reaching out to give it a little push.

"Let's keep looking around," I said. "I saw one in New York that I just loved, and it's supposed to be here." We strolled around, looking at everything. An amazing variety of artwork was in that one little gallery. We saw sculptures carved out of wood, and sculptures that had been cast in bronze. We saw pieces made out of what looked like old car parts, and pieces chiseled in marble. Some were brightly painted, and others were the natural color of aging metal or wood.

We touched almost every sculpture. Some of them moved, tilting or rocking on their bases. Others stayed put, but it was still a pleasure to be able to feel the materials they were made of. I noticed a man and a little boy — his son, I guess — touching all the sculptures, too. You don't have to be an art expert to love Don Newman's sculptures.

"I really do like this stuff," said Stacey. "Not all of it — some of it's a little weird for me, and I feel like I don't understand it. But most of it is really cool."

"I'm glad you like it," I said. "I thought you would." We were walking as we talked. Suddenly, we turned a corner, and there it was. "Daphne!" I cried.

"Who?" asked Stacey, looking around.

"Daphne," I repeated. "It's a sculpture. The one I saw in New York." I walked over to it. "I just love this one," I said. "Somehow it makes me feel calm and peaceful."

"I see what you mean," said Stacey. "It gives me the same feeling." She reached out to touch it. "Oh, cool," she said. "Look how it moves."

I ran my hand over it. It rocked gently on its base. I touched it again. Then I stood back from it, frowning.

"What's the matter?" Stacey asked.

I paused for a second, and then shrugged. "I'm not sure," I said. "Maybe nothing. It just seems . . . different."

"Different from when you saw it in New York?" Stacey asked.

"Uh-huh," I answered. But I couldn't really say *how* it was different. I looked at it more closely. Had it been damaged?

"That was quite a while ago, wasn't it?" asked Stacey.

"Well, yes," I said, thinking hard. "But — Stace, you're going to think I'm crazy, but I have a feeling this statue is a fake!"

"You're right," said Stacey.

"I am?" I asked. "You think it's a fake, too?"

"No," she replied, grinning at me. "I think you're crazy."

"Thanks a lot," I said, grinning back at her. "But really, Stacey, something's wrong here. Not just with this piece, either. Something strange is going on at this museum. I mean, first the robbery, and now this."

"I don't know, Claud," said Stacey. "I think you're imagining things."

"I didn't imagine the robbery," I said stubbornly. "And I'm not imagining this, either." I rocked the statue again. "Something is definitely weird about this sculpture."

"Okay, so what if something weird *is* going on?" asked Stacey. "What can *we* do about it?"

"We can talk to the curator," I replied promptly. "That's what we'll do, talk to the curator," I added again, more firmly.

"Claud, are you sure?" asked Stacey. But I wasn't listening to her. I was walking quickly back through the gallery toward the museum offices, which are off the main lobby. Stacey followed behind me.

"I need to see the curator," I told the receptionist, when we arrived in the outer office.

"Do you have an appointment?" she asked, "Mr. Snipes is a very busy man, and he doesn't usually see people on Saturdays."

"I'm sure he's busy and I don't have an appointment," I said, "but this is a very important matter. I have to see him as soon as possible." My voice was growing louder. Stacey stuck by my side, but she didn't say anything.

"I don't think — " began the receptionist, but just then a door opened behind her and a man stuck his head out.

"What's going on, Ms. Hobbes?" asked the man. He was a skinny guy, dressed in a black suit. He looked more like an insurance agent than a curator. He had black hair and a thin black mustache and very pale skin.

"These girls wanted to see you," she said, "but I told them — "

"What seems to be the problem?" Mr. Snipes asked, interrupting her. He looked at me intently, and I noticed his small, dark eyes.

"If I could just speak to you for five minutes," I began.

"Yes?" he said impatiently. He gestured toward his office, and Stacey and I followed him in.

He sat down behind his desk. Stacey and I stood in front of it. Suddenly I remembered my fantasy — Mr. Snipes asking me to show my art in his museum — and I blushed.

"Well, it — it's just that I noticed something strange about one of the Don Newman pieces," I said finally. I told Mr. Snipes that I had seen — and touched — the sculpture before, and that it seemed different now. "Maybe somebody switched it during the robbery. I just think it may be a fake, I mean, a forgery," I finished, looking at the floor. Somehow I knew he wasn't going to believe me.

I was right. "This is the most absurd thing I've ever heard," he said, rolling his eyes. He pushed a button on his intercom. "Ms. Hobbes, bring me the Newman file," he said into it. Then he looked back at Stacey and me. "Playing detective may be an amusing way to pass an afternoon," he said, "but taking up *my* time with your ridiculous theories is pushing things too far." Ms. Hobbes brought in the file, and he showed me the registration number for the sculpture. Then he marched us down to the gallery and showed us that the number matched the one on the artwork. Afterward, we went back to his office. "I hope you've enjoyed your little game," he said. "And I trust I won't be seeing you in here again."

"No, sir. We're very sorry, sir," said Stacey.

I didn't say anything. I was too busy sneaking a piece of paper off of the desk while Stacey apologized. It was a copy of Mr. Snipes' resume. I saw several lying there, and I had been overcome by the need to know more about this nasty man. I know it wasn't the *right* thing to do, but right or not, I had to do it. I was so happy to have this new museum to go to,

and I wasn't about to let some crooked curator spoil things for me — or for the kids of
Stoneybrook. Something rotten was going on
in that museum, and I wanted to get to the
bottom of it.

CHAPTER 8

I didn't sleep well at all that Saturday night. I guess I was preoccupied with trying to work out a solution to the museum mystery. I kept tossing and turning, trying to figure out what was different about that sculpture and how it could be tied to the coin robbery. I just *knew* they were related, somehow.

First thing Sunday morning, Kristy called me. "How about if we all come over this afternoon to talk about the mystery?" she asked. "I've been thinking and thinking, and I haven't come up with any answers. Maybe if we get together we can make some progress."

Of course, Kristy already knew what had happened the day before, after she and the others had left Stacey and me at the museum. I had called the BSC members and told them about our visit with Mr. Snipes. But I had left out one detail. I hadn't said anything about swiping that resume. I guess I was a little ashamed of myself for doing it. In fact, I had decided to throw it away and pretend I had never seen it.

I told Kristy that a meeting sounded great. "I'll make some raspberry brownies," I said. "And some popcorn, too, for Stacey. "

After we hung up, I headed downstairs for breakfast. "Morning, honey," said my mother, who was sitting at the table eating waffles. My dad was at the stove, cooking them. That's his Sunday morning project.

"Any left for me?" I asked.

"Coming right up," he said. He poured some batter into the waffle iron.

I picked up the local paper and began to read it. I scanned all the articles in the news section, but I didn't see one word about the robbery. I wondered if the police were even taking the case seriously.

After I had baked the brownies for my friends, I spent the rest of the morning working on a small clay sculpture I had started before I saw the Don Newman show. I had been happy with it two days ago. But now, after I'd seen a professional artist's work, it looked lumpy and uninspired. I smushed it into a ball and started over again.

Before I knew it, it was time for our "meeting." Kristy arrived first, as usual. I heard her thumping up the stairs, and I barely had time to whisk Mr. Snipes' resume into my desk drawer.

Kristy had barely settled herself in the director's chair when Mary Anne and Logan showed up. "I brought him along," said Mary Anne, pulling Logan into the room, "even though he didn't really want to come."

"I had a basketball game planned for this afternoon," said Logan, "but Mary Anne convinced me this was more important." Mary Anne sat down on my bed and patted the spot next to her.

"Sit here, Logan," she said.

Logan blushed and shook his head. Sometimes he has a hard time being in a room full of girls, and sitting on a bed next to his girlfriend would only make him more uncomfortable. He sat on the floor, instead, and I sat beside Mary Anne.

Jessi and Mal showed up next, with Stacey right behind them.

"Any news?" asked Stacey, raising her eyebrows at me.

"You mean, did Mr. Snipes call to say I was right and the statue was a fake?" I asked, grinning. "Nope. Sorry to disappoint you."

"Mr. Snipes was kind of creepy," said Stacey. "I didn't like the way he talked to you. It was like he was the king and you were a peasant or something."

"Condescending," Mallory murmured.

"What?" I asked.

"Condescending," she said again. "That's the way he was talking to you. In a condescending manner. It means he was acting superior." Mal kind of collects words. I guess it's because she wants to be a writer some day.

"Speaking of acting," said Mary Anne, with a giggle, "wait till you guys hear about the video that Claire made yesterday." She and Mallory told us about Claire's big show business debut.

"The amazing thing," Mal said, after they had told us about their day at the mall, "is that the video is really pretty good. I should know, since I've been forced to watch it at least fifty times already." She rolled her eyes. "I mean, I'm sick of it already, but I do have to admit that Claire has some talent."

"Maybe she should go on *Star Search* or something," said Logan.

"Please!" exclaimed Mallory, rolling her eyes again. "Don't put any ideas in her head."

We all cracked up.

"Okay," said Kristy, sitting up in her chair. "Let's get down to business. We're here to talk about the museum mystery."

"Right," I said. "So what do we do next?"

"I think we have to find out more about Mr. Snipes," said Stacey. "I have a feeling he's involved in the robbery somehow."

"But he's the curator of the museum!" said Jessi.

"I know," said Stacey. "I just think he's up to no good."

"What can we do, though?" asked Logan. "We need to find out more about him, but how?"

I was practically biting my tongue. His resume was sitting right there in my desk drawer, and it would tell us a lot. But I knew I had been wrong to take it, and I felt embarrassed.

"Yeah, how?" asked Kristy. "I mean, we can't exactly march into the museum office and ask for his resume!"

That did it. "We don't have to," I said. I stood up, opened my desk drawer, and pulled out the paper I had swiped. "I have it right here."

"Whoa!" said Stacey, taking a look at it. "Where did you get that?"

"From his desk, yesterday," I said, blushing. "I took it when nobody was looking."

"Claud! You could have gotten into a lot of trouble for that," said Mary Anne.

"Only if she had gotten caught," said Kristy,

"and she didn't." She leaned over my shoulder to look at it. "This is perfect!" she said. "Look, it lists every museum he's ever worked at."

I relaxed. Nobody was calling me a thief or a criminal.

"It's kind of weird that it was on his desk," mused Mallory. "I mean, the museum just opened. Is he looking for another job already?"

"Maybe he is," said Logan. "Maybe he wants to get out of there, now that there's been a robbery."

We talked for awhile about Mr. Snipes and why he might want to leave the museum. Then we decided to head for the library to see what we could learn about the other museums he had worked for.

I may not be great at schoolwork, but I *do* know how to use the library, since my mom works there. The library's only open for a few hours on Sundays, so we had to work fast. We worked with the Readers' Guide to Periodicals, hunting for articles about the museums on Mr. Snipes' resume. Soon we had a whole page full of notes. When the librarian brought us the magazines we had requested, we divided them up and began to read.

"This is amazing," said Mal. "I've already

found two articles about robberies that took place at this museum in Texas. And they happened when Mr. Snipes was the curator there."

"Same thing with this museum in Oregon," I said. "They had the biggest art robbery that had ever taken place in that state. And guess who was the curator?"

"Nothing on the museum in California," said Mary Anne. "It just says that Mr. Snipes bought a lot of paintings that completed their collection."

"But this museum in New Jersey was robbed when he was there," said Kristy, sounding excited. "The thieves got away with thousands of dollars worth of antiquities. What are *antiquities*?"

"Old stuff," said Mallory. "Valuable old stuff."

"We should go to the police," said Stacey. "It's obvious that this guy is a criminal. I mean, robberies happened in three out of the four museums he worked at."

"I don't know," said Kristy thoughtfully. "I mean, we don't actually have *evidence* that he was involved in all these robberies. Maybe he just has bad luck."

"Maybe, but I doubt it," I said. Personally, I was feeling kind of happy about finding all this evidence. I was glad I had swiped the resume. I *knew* that guy was sinister. And now we practically had *proof* he was an art thief.

Practically. Not really, though. Kristy was right. It wasn't time to go to the police. Not yet. Not until we were positive.

CHAPTER 9

Tuesday

Boy, Mal, you weren't kidding about "Claire and her "quest for stardom." I thought it was all a big joke, but now I see that she's very serious about it. She really wants to have a show business career. The only thing is, I'm not exactly sure she's going about it in the right way...

"Hey, Kristy!" Adam jumped out of a tree in the Pikes' yard as Kristy dashed up the front walk. Jordan and Byron were right behind him.

"We're going to build a tree fort," said Jordan importantly. "It's going to be like a castle, with towers and places to pour boiling oil out of, and we're going to dig a moat around the bottom of the tree, too!"

"Plus we're going to hang a big flag from it," added Adam. "It's going to tell the name of our club and say that no girls are allowed."

"But we'll let *you* up in it," said Byron generously. "There's going to be a rope ladder, and we'll let you climb it."

"It sounds great," said Kristy. "Do you already have all your wood and nails and everything?"

"Wood?" asked Byron.

"Nails?" asked Adam.

"Well, no," said Jordan, "but as soon as the plans are ready, then we'll get the stuff we need to build it. It's going to be awesome!"

The triplets climbed back up into the tree. Kristy smiled. She wondered if they would actually build the tree house. It almost didn't matter, since planning it was obviously as much fun as playing in it.

Kristy rang the doorbell. She was looking forward to her sitting job that day, watching four of the Pike kids. The triplets would be going to soccer practice, which left Vanessa, Margo, Nicky, and Claire in Kristy's care. Mal wasn't sitting for them that day — she was taking it easy, since she hadn't been feeling well.

"Kristy's here!" yelled Claire, flinging the door open. "Hi, Kristy-silly-billy-goo-goo!"

"Hi, Claire, you little bear," said Kristy playfully.

"Hi, Kristy," said Margo, following Claire into the hallway. "Did Claire tell you yet?"

"Tell me what?" asked Kristy.

"*You* tell her," said Claire, suddenly shy.

"No, *you*," said Margo.

"*I'll* tell her," said Nicky, who had just joined them. He was holding a sandwich — peanut butter on a pumpernickel bagel. He took a big bite. "Wfmph vronna ghaf uh schoe," he said.

"*What?*" Kristy asked.

"He said we're going to have a show," explained Margo.

"A show!" echoed Claire, looking *very* excited. "And we're going to invite all the neighbors."

"A show?" repeated Kristy. "I didn't know

you guys had been rehearsing a show. Mal didn't mention it. You're inviting the neighborhood over?"

Margo nodded.

"When are you planning to put on this show?" asked Kristy, hoping it wouldn't be for a week or so.

"Today," said Margo.

"*Today?* This afternoon?" Kristy groaned.

Just then, Mrs. Pike came bustling into the room. "I've got to run," she said to Kristy. "Thanks for being on time. I'll be back by six."

"Fine," said Kristy. "Oh, uh, Mrs. Pike?" She wanted to ask Mrs. Pike whether the kids could put on their show, but Mrs. Pike was on her way out the door, calling to the triplets. She didn't hear Kristy at all.

"Let's go, boys!" called Mrs. Pike. "If you want a ride to soccer practice you have to come right now. Otherwise you can walk." The triplets made a break for the car. Mrs. Pike waved to Kristy and the other kids as she climbed in and started the engine.

"Bye," said Kristy, almost to herself. Now the issue of the show was up to her. Mal was napping, and she didn't want to wake her up just to ask her opinion. She turned to Margo. "Where's Vanessa? Is she in your show?"

Margo nodded. "I think so. She was upstairs in her room writing something for it. A 'poetic interlude,' she called it. Something like that."

"Oh, dear," said Kristy, imagining Vanessa reading an epic poem as all the neighbors watched politely. "Tell me more about what you're planning," she said. "Is there going to be singing? Dancing? Are you going to put on skits?"

Margo and Nicky exchanged looks. "It's just a show," said Margo. "It'll be fun, we promise. And it's all ready."

"Please can we do it?" begged Claire. "Please?"

"Well, I guess it'll be all right if everyone stays outdoors," said Kristy, figuring that if the actors — or the audience — got wild they would be better off outside where things wouldn't get broken.

"No!" howled Claire. "It can't be outside. It has to be in the rec room!"

"Claire's right," said Margo. "It has to be inside."

"We can fit a lot of people in there," said Nicky thoughtfully. "I figured it out once. That room can probably hold fifty people. As long as some of them are kids, that is."

"Fifty people?" said Kristy, shocked. "No way, José. We are not going to crowd fifty people into your rec room to see something you just planned today." She envisioned a huge audience making a commotion when they were forced to watch an unrehearsed mess of a show.

"How many can we have?" asked Nicky. "Twenty?"

"No, not twenty," said Kristy. She thought fast. "How about five?"

"Five!" said Margo. "That's hardly any people at all. Let us have ten."

"Eight," said Kristy firmly. "That's final. You can have your show in the rec room, and you can invite eight people."

The kids saw that Kristy was serious, and that there would be no more bargaining. They huddled together, planning who to invite. "I'll go over to the Barretts'," said Nicky. "I bet Mrs. Barrett will bring Buddy and Suzy and Marnie."

"That's four people," said Margo, counting on her fingers. "I'll go to the Braddocks'. Matt's probably at soccer practice, but maybe Haley and her mom can come. That makes six. Who else should we ask?"

"Marilyn and Carolyn!" said Claire. "I bet they'll come."

"Fine," said Kristy. "I'll go with you to ask them, since you'll have to cross the street to get to their house. But first I'm going to let Vanessa know where we'll be." She ran upstairs and found Vanessa hard at work.

"Want to hear my poem?" asked Vanessa.

"I think it's an especially good one. It begins, "Welcome to our show, people in the know."

"Um, I'd love to," said Kristy. "But I don't really have time now." She told Vanessa where she was going. "I guess I'll just have to hear it when everybody else does." She edged out the door, relieved to have an excuse. Vanessa's poems can be very long.

Kristy and Claire headed for the Arnolds' while Margo went to the Braddocks' and Nicky went to the Barretts'. A half hour later, everyone was assembled in the rec room. Mrs. Braddock hadn't been able to come, but Mrs. Arnold had taken her place. Nicky seated everyone carefully, with the smaller kids in front so everyone would be able to see. Margo pretended to collect tickets. Claire disappeared to put on her costume and fetch Vanessa.

Finally, the kids were ready to start. "Ladles and gentlebeans," said Nicky, grinning. He bowed and swept off the baseball cap he was wearing as Master of Ceremonies. "I welcome you to the show of the century. You've never seen anything like it, and you probably never will." There was polite applause. "May I introduce our first performer, Vanessa Pike. The poet of Slate Street!"

Vanessa stood in front of the audience, holding a flower in one hand and a thick wad of papers in the other. "I have composed a poem for the occasion," she said. "The first section is about today's performance." She took a deep breath and began to read.

After Vanessa had read four pages, Kristy realized the audience was growing restless. She motioned to Nicky, who cut off Vanessa in the middle of a rhyme. "And now for our next guest," he said, hustling Vanessa off the "stage," "I introduce Margo the marionette."

Margo was now dressed in a clown outfit that was, Kristy remembered, left over from Halloween. She performed a jerky dance that lasted about ten seconds, bowed, and ran off the stage. The audience applauded, but Kristy noticed that some of its older members were looking a little bewildered.

"And now," said Nicky, "for the centerpiece of today's show." Claire skipped to the front of the room. "A super-special movie featuring our own Claire Pike!" Claire bent down and turned on the TV. Then she pressed "play" on the VCR, and a picture came on. It was Claire, dressed as Dorothy, standing on the Yellow Brick Road.

Kristy told me later that it was as if a light bulb went on over her head as soon as Claire reached for the VCR. "I should have known," Kristy said. "The entire afternoon was just an excuse for Claire to show off her video."

Luckily, the audience didn't seem to feel

tricked. After all, they hadn't paid anything. And Claire's video wasn't bad. In fact, it was fun to watch, said Kristy. But after the audience left, Kristy felt that she should give Claire a little Talk.

"Claire," she said, "if you want to show people your video, that's fine. But let them know what they're in for, next time."

Claire hung her head. "I will," she said. "It's just that I want lots of people to see it. That way I might get discovered."

Kristy wondered who Claire had thought she would get discovered *by*. Carolyn Arnold? She shook her head and gave Claire a hug. "*I* think you're a star," she said. Then she stood up. "Come on. Let's fix a snack for all the performers."

CHAPTER 10

"Somewhere, over the rainbow," I hummed to myself as I walked up to the Pikes' front door. The song was on my mind because I was on my way to a baby-sitting job, and one of the kids I would be sitting for was Claire. It was Wednesday afternoon, and Mal and I were going to sit for her brothers and sisters. I was looking forward to the job; I had been spending so much time thinking about the museum mystery that I was ready to take a break and just baby-sit.

Kristy had called me the night before to tell me about the "show" the kids had put on. "Watch out," she warned me. "Claire has a one-track mind these days. I don't think she'll be happy until she wins an Oscar for that video." Kristy laughed. "Actually, it's kind of cute," she said. "And who knows? Maybe we *will* see her on the Academy Awards some-day."

"That'll be the day," I said, giggling. I was picturing five-year-old Claire in a formal gown. She was trailing across the stage, accepting the Oscar statue graciously (it would be nearly as big as she was!), then standing and acknowledging the applause of the audience. I told Kristy about the image, and she laughed, too.

"I guess it's just a phase," said Kristy. "But Claire is taking herself pretty seriously, so don't let her catch you giggling at her."

"No way," I said. "I've had dreams of fame myself, so I know how it is." I remembered my fantasy about being asked to show my art at the Stoneybrook Museum.

Anyway, as I was saying, I was humming to myself as I approached the Pikes' front porch. And when I knocked on the door, guess who answered it? Right. Claire did. And what do you think she said. Hello? No.

"Come see my video!" Claire pulled me inside and led me toward the rec room.

"Video?" I asked, pretending I didn't know anything about it. I wanted to give Claire the fun of telling me. "What video?"

"My superstar video," said Claire, jumping up and down with excitement. "Wait till you see it!" She had hit the rewind button on the VCR and she was jumping around some more while she waited. "I'm going to be famous soon," she said. "As famous as Michael Jackson! As famous as Roseanne! As famous as Ms. Stotler!"

"Who's Ms. Stotler?" I asked. The name sounded vaguely familiar, but I couldn't place it.

"She's the principal," said Nicky disgustedly. He had come into the room and flopped down on the couch. "Claire thinks she's famous just because she's the principal of our school."

"She *is* famous," said Claire. "Right, Claudia?"

"Sure," I said. "In a way. Not in the same way as Michael Jackson, though."

"I know that," said Claire, pouting a little. We heard a click from the VCR. "It's ready!" Claire cried. She ran to the door of the rec room. "Everybody! Come and see the show! Claudia's here, and she asked me to play it for her."

I raised my eyebrows. I didn't remember asking her, but that didn't really matter. I watched as, one by one, Claire's brothers and sisters straggled into the room.

Vanessa sat on the couch, next to Nicky. She had brought a book along, and she immediately opened it and began to read. Adam, Jordan, and Byron plopped down on the floor. Margo and Mal came in last. Mal sat down next to me. "Are you ready for this?" she whispered.

"Sure," I said. "But why are you all watching it again? You must have seen it a million times."

"We have," she replied with a sigh. "And we're sick of it. But Claire throws a huge tantrum if we refuse to watch, so it's easier just to sit through it again."

I nodded. "Well, Claire," I said, "it looks like everybody's here. Why don't you play it?"

"First I have to give a little speech about it," said Claire. Her brothers and sisters groaned, but Claire ignored them. She stood up straighter and smiled professionally. "This tape that you're about to see showcases a new and wonderful talent," she said. "Ladies and gentlemen, please welcome Miss Claire Pike!" She waited for us to applaud.

"Vanessa wrote the speech for her," Mal whispered to me. "She says it every time now, before she plays the tape."

Claire bent over and pressed the play button, and the tape came on. I glanced around the room and noticed that nobody was paying much attention. Vanessa was reading her book. The triplets were wrestling quietly on the floor. Nicky was picking at a scab on his knee. Margo was trying to braid one of her pigtails. And Mal had closed her eyes and seemed to be taking a nap. But Claire didn't notice. She was focused on the TV screen, watching closely. I watched, too.

Claire didn't look exactly like Dorothy, but she looked close enough. And she didn't sing quite as well as Judy Garland (who plays Dorothy in the movie), but I have to say that her voice was better than I had expected. And she did a really good job acting out the song, looking particularly wistful when she sang the part about bluebirds flying over the rainbow.

When the tape ended, I clapped as hard as I could. The kids clapped, too, but only once or twice each. They weren't exactly enthusiastic, and I couldn't blame them.

But Claire didn't notice. "Thank you, thank you," she said, curtsying graciously.

"Can we go now?" asked Jordan. He and the triplets stood up and left, and Nicky followed them.

"So did you like it?" Claire asked me. "Did you notice the part where I looked up, like I was looking at a rainbow?"

"I liked it very much," I said.

"Can you discover me?" Claire asked hopefully.

"You mean, can I help you get famous?" I asked. "I don't think so. I don't know any important people or anything."

"How am I ever going to be discovered?" asked Claire. "Nobody important is ever going to come to my rec room."

She was right. I didn't know what to say. "I guess you can't become famous unless you have an agent," I said, thinking of articles I had read about stars.

"An agent?" asked Claire. "What's that?"

"Somebody who helps you get acting jobs," explained Mal. "I don't know how you find one, though."

I was thinking fast. "I do!" I said. "I mean, I know somebody who would know, anyway. She has an agent, herself."

"Who?" asked Claire. "Can I meet her?"

"Her name is Rosie Wilder," I said. "I used to baby-sit for her a lot. She was always trying out for acting jobs, and I know that her agent found her some jobs in TV commercials."

"Rosie Wilder," said Mal thoughtfully. "Wasn't she always taking a million lessons?"

"Yup," I replied, "but I think she eased up a little. It was kind of overwhelming." Stardom can be hard on kids. We actually know one other kid who is on TV, and it hasn't always been easy for him, either. His name is Derek Masters, and he's a really nice boy. I would have asked him to help with Claire's career, but he was out in California making a TV show called *P.S. 162*. He's practically the star of that show, which is about an inner-city school. "Why don't I call Rosie," I said, "and see if she can help us?"

"Yeah!" cried Claire. "Do it right now! Please!"

I dialed Rosie's number. I didn't think she would answer the phone herself, since she is usually so busy with her lessons, but she picked up the phone on the second ring. Then I told her about Claire, and asked if she could help.

"I'd be glad to," Rosie answered, sounding more mature than her seven years. "I have tap class in an hour, but I'll be home until then. Come on over, and tell Claire to bring her video."

Margo and Vanessa decided that they wanted to come along and meet Rosie the star, so Mal said she would stay home with the boys while I took the girls to Rosie's. Claire removed her video from the VCR and put it carefully into its case. She clutched it to her chest all the way to Rosie's.

Rosie answered the door, and I introduced the kids to each other. "I know your brother Nicky," Rosie said to the girls. "He's in my class at school." (Rosie skipped a grade.) She led us upstairs to her bedroom. "My mom said we could watch the video in here," she explained. "She's doing some work downstairs."

"You have your own TV in your room?" asked Margo, awed.

"Sure," said Rosie. "My own VCR, too."

"Lucky duck," said Margo enviously.

Claire was looking around the room, wide-eyed. "Are these pictures all of you?" she asked. Framed photographs lined the walls. There was Rosie on the set of a carpet-cleaner commercial, and Rosie playing violin in an orchestra. Claire pointed to one of Rosie singing in a recital. "Weren't you nervous?" she asked.

Rosie shrugged. "Not really," she said. "I'm used to it. Why don't you give me your video?"

Claire handed it over a little reluctantly. She seemed suddenly shy. Rosie stuck the video into the VCR, pressed play, and stood back to watch. She was silent until the video ended. Claire, who looked nervous now, waited for her comments.

"Not bad," said Rosie thoughtfully. "Not bad at all, for an amateur." She put a finger to her cheek and thought. "I'm sure you could find an agent if you sent this around. I would even tell you to send it to my agent, but I happen to know she's not taking on any new clients these days."

"How do I find out where to send it?" asked Claire. Now she looked happy and excited.

"I'll give you some addresses," said Rosie. "Then, the best thing to do would be to copy the video and send it out to everybody at once. That'll save time." She sat down at her desk and made a list of agents for Claire. "Here," she said. "Good luck!"

When we left Rosie's, Claire was practically bubbling over with enthusiasm. "This is it!" she said. "I'm going to get discovered for sure now." She skipped along happily.

I knew that copying the video would be expensive, so I talked Claire into sending it to one agent at a time, starting with the first one on Rosie's list. And that's what she did, with my help and Mal's, as soon as she got home. I thought we should wait and check with Mrs. Pike about whether it was all right to send it, but Mal said it was okay. Claire dictated a note to me, packed up the video, and gave it to me to take to the post office. I had a feeling she would be watching the mailbox every minute until she got a reply. Claire was sure she was bound for stardom.

CHAPTER 11

As soon as Mrs. Pike came home that afternoon, Mal and I headed over to my house for our BSC meeting. By running most of the way, we arrived before Kristy did. *Just* before. She came pounding up the stairs right after us. "Where's everybody else?" she asked, impatiently. "I had a great idea on the way over here."

Mal and I let out big fake groans and rolled our eyes. I can't tell you how many times I've heard those words — "I had a great idea" — come out of Kristy's mouth. And usually, her ideas really *are* great. But we still like to tease her once in awhile.

"It's only five twenty-five," I said, in answer to her question. "They'll be here in time for our meeting, I'm sure." And I was right. Two minutes later Shannon and Stacey arrived, with Jessi and Mary Anne behind them. "See?" I said to Kristy with a grin. I held out

93

a package of Twizzlers. "Relax and have one of these," I added. "Then you can tell us about your idea."

I passed a bag of Ruffles around the other way, and handed a bag of pretzels to Stacey.

"Any news on the museum robbery?" Stacey asked.

I shook my head. "Nothing," I said. "But I think about it all the time. I *know* I'll come up with something soon."

"Ahem," said Kristy, pointing to the clock. It had just clicked to 5:30. "This meeting is now called to order."

Our meeting began the way they always do. We talked about recent news on our clients (Mal and I reported on Claire and her videotape) and about scheduling problems and stuff like that. I can't tell you any specifics, because after a couple of minutes, I kind of tuned out. Stacey's question had made me think about the museum mystery again. *Why* couldn't I figure it out? I felt as if I weren't remembering something right, or as if some fact were missing. And if I could just find that one fact, everything would come together and the mystery would be solved. I decided to go over the case again, starting from the beginning and remembering every single detail. I saw myself entering the museum with Corrie and Marilyn and Carolyn. In my mind, I walked through all the exhibits we had seen.

The phone rang, jolting me out of my thoughts. Kristy answered it and talked for a few minutes to Mrs. Pike, who was asking for a sitter for the next day. Then Mary Anne checked the record book to see who was available. I knew I wasn't, so I tuned out once more and went back to my first visit to the museum.

The Science Room. The Discovery Room. The Music Room. I couldn't recall anything strange happening in any of those places. I moved on, and remembered the sound of the fire alarm and how responsible I had felt for my charges. That was the point at which things had become exciting, so I tried extra hard to concentrate on the facts.

Just as I was picturing the courtyard we had been herded into after the second bell rang, Kristy spoke up. "Okay, so as I was telling Claud and Mal," she said, "I had this great idea."

This time, everybody in the room groaned and rolled their eyes. Kristy pretended to be mad, but I knew she thought it was funny, too.

"Why don't you tell us about it?" asked Mary Anne supportively.

"Well," said Kristy, and she launched into

some complicated scheme for keeping better records of how many hours we work every week. Guess what I did while she was talking? I tuned out. I went back to that day at the museum. I pictured myself walking into the building, and down a hall. I saw myself peeking into the room where the coin case had been broken. What was it about that case?

"Whoa!" I said.

"What?" asked Kristy. Apparently I had interrupted her in the middle of a sentence. She looked annoyed.

"Nothing," I said. She began to talk again, and I concentrated on the image of that room with the broken case. I made myself look at it again. I tried to picture it exactly.

"That's it!" I shouted suddenly. "Oh, my lord!"

"What?" Kristy asked again. "Claudia, I'm in the middle of an idea here."

"I know, and I'm really, really sorry. But I just thought of something. Something really important about the museum mystery."

"Ooh, tell us!" said Mal. Kristy's lastest great idea couldn't compete with the museum mystery. Everybody was looking at me, eager to hear what I had to say.

"Okay," I said. "Remember the glass case that had been broken into? The one that used to have the coins in it?" My friends nodded.

"Well, here's the thing. I was trying to remember exactly how it looked, and I realized something. I saw broken glass *covering* the inside of the case. If somebody had broken the case to steal the coins, the glass would have sprinkled all over the coins. Then, when the thief picked them up, there would have been little round bare spots where the coins had been. Do you see what I mean?" Again, everyone nodded.

"But there weren't any bare spots," I continued. "So that means somebody must have taken the coins *before* the glass was broken. Somebody who had a key. Like maybe the curator? Anyway, the thief must have broken the glass *after* he took the coins, to make it look like a robbery by somebody who didn't have a key. But it was an inside job. I'm sure of it." I leaned back and crossed my arms. "That's it. What do you think?"

"Wow!" exclaimed Mal.

"Awesome," said Jessi.

"Good thinking, Claud," said Kristy, who seemed to have forgiven me for interrupting her.

"And your parents think that reading Nancy Drew rots your brain," said Stacey, giggling. "Obviously, you've learned a lot from those books."

We never did get back to Kristy's great idea.

We talked about the museum mystery for the rest of the meeting.

That night, I tried to study for a math test. But I couldn't concentrate. All I could think about was the museum. What if there really *was* a thief on the museum staff? Was Don Newman's work safe? I would feel awful if any of his sculptures were stolen. For that matter, maybe one of them already *had* been stolen. I remembered how Daphne had felt so strange to me. Sure, the curator had "proven" to me that it wasn't a fake, but I just didn't trust him.

I thought and thought, and I became more and more worried. Shouldn't Don Newman know there was funny business going on at the museum? Maybe he would want to pull his pieces out and keep them in a safer place. Suddenly, almost before I knew what I was doing, I reached for the phone and called Information. "Newman," I told the operator. "Don Newman." She gave me the number, and I dialed it without a pause. My heart pounded as the phone rang once, twice, three times. What was I *doing*?

"Hello?" A man's voice was on the other end.

"Um, Mr. Newman?" I said, trying to keep my voice from shaking.

"That's me," he said. (He sounded friend-

ly.) "What can I do for you?"

"My name is Claudia Kishi," I told him. "I — I really love your work."

"Well, thank you, Claudia Kishi. That's always a pleasure to hear."

I relaxed a little. I began to tell him why I had called. I crossed my fingers, hoping he wouldn't think I was some kind of nut. And you know what? He didn't. He treated me like an adult, not a kid. He thanked me for my concern. And he told me a wonderful secret.

"I think I may know why Daphne felt different to you," he said. "You see, back when I created that sculpture, I had two small children. They're almost grown now, but at the time they were very young. I liked to involve them in my art, partly because it helped keep them occupied while I was working. So I created hiding places in my sculptures. Places where I could put little toys for them to find." He paused for a second, as if remembering. "I had almost forgotten about that. They loved looking for their surprises. It was fun for all three of us. Anyway, maybe I left one of the toys inside Daphne, and that's what you were feeling."

"That is so cool," I said. I was thrilled to hear such a personal detail from a famous artist. "You must be a wonderful father." Then

I paused for a second. "But there's still one thing I don't understand. Unless you put in a toy or took one out in the past year or so, Daphne would have felt the same to me both times I touched it. And it didn't. It felt different. I still think something may be wrong." I was embarrassed to be pushing my point, but I felt strongly about it.

"I'll tell you what," said Mr. Newman. "I'll be at the museum myself in a couple of days, and I'll check Daphne then. You've made me curious. In fact, I wish I could go there tomorrow, but I'll be out of town."

I sighed. I was grateful to him for taking me seriously, and I told him so.

"Well, this is serious business," he answered, "and I want to thank you for telling me about it. Listen, the museum is having a big formal party for the closing of my show on Friday night. Why don't you come? That's when I'll be able to check on Daphne. We can do it together."

"Oh!" I said. I was so surprised that I didn't know what else to say. This was the party I had dreamed about going to, and now I had been personally invited by the artist himself! Finally I recovered. "I'd love to," I told him. "But I don't know if my parents will let me."

"Bring them along," he said. "I look forward to meeting them — and you."

After I hung up, I drifted downstairs, feeling as if I were walking on clouds. I told my parents about the invitation, and my father said he would be happy to go to the party with me. (I didn't tell them about the detective work I was doing. In fact, I told a little white lie about having called Don Newman for a school project. I didn't know how else to explain the invitation.)

I floated back upstairs and tried to study again. But before long I had jumped up to look through my closet. I had been invited to a formal party, and I only had two days to figure out what to wear. This was going to take some thought.

CHAPTER 12

Thursday

Well, I think Claire came face to face with reality today, and it looks like her *A Star Is Born* phase may be coming to an end. Poor Claire, but what a relief. Right, Mal?

Note to Claudia:

Remind me to tell you important news I found out about the museum.

On Thursday afternoon, Jessi and Mal sat for the Pike kids. It was a bright, sunny day, fortunately, which meant that the triplets, Nicky, and Margo were playing outside. Vanessa was curled up in an armchair with her nose in a book (her usual pose), and Claire was trying on different "audition outfits" and asking Mal and Jessi's opinion on each one.

"This is the glamorous look," she said, trailing a pink feather boa down the stairs. She wore a spangled tutu which Mal had worn in a first grade play (it's a little ratty by now, since all the Pike girls have used it for dressing up), white high heels swiped from her mother's closet, and a pair of red sunglasses pushed up on her head.

"Very nice," said Jessi. "But maybe just a little too — what's the word?" she paused. "Um, too glitzy, maybe? The agent might like it if you looked more like a regular girl."

Claire nodded and ran back upstairs to change. She came back down in a few minutes, dressed in her best pink dress with lace trim. She was still wearing the high heels, and the sunglasses were still perched on her head. "I don't want to look *too* regular," she announced. "How's this?"

Jessi and Mal exchanged looks and tried not to giggle. "Fine," said Mal. "Just fine."

Claire curtsied. "Thank you, ladies and gentlemen," she said.

This time, Mal and Jessi were unable to contain their giggles, but Claire didn't seem to notice. "Can I call Rosie?" she asked. "I want to ask her some more questions. Plus, she said she would show me her tap shoes the next time I came over. So can I call?"

"How about if I call for you?" asked Jessi. She didn't want Rosie to feel pestered by Claire. She dialed the Wilders' number, and Mrs. Wilder answered. It turned out that Rosie was busy with a violin lesson. "And tomorrow her voice teacher will be here," said Mrs. Wilder. "Perhaps Rosie should call you back when she has some free time."

"Boo!" said Claire, when Jessi told her how busy Rosie was. "I want to talk to her some more. Why does she have to take so many dumb lessons, anyway?"

"That's just how it is, when you're in show business," explained Jessi. "I know, since I'm a dancer. I take classes all the time. I have to, if I want to be a professional ballerina someday."

"But you already know how to dance ballet," said Claire. "I've seen you do it."

"That's true, but I still have a lot to learn," said Jessi. "Being in show business can keep a person very busy. It's not an easy life."

"What do you mean?" asked Claire. She snuggled up next to Jessi on the couch. "Tell me."

So, Mal went outside to watch her sister and brothers while Jessi told Claire about the life of a professional entertainer. She told her about the lessons that actors and dancers and singers have to take. "Even when they're stars, they still take lessons," said Jessi. She told her about auditions, and how nerve-wracking they can be. "Sometimes they reject people just because they're too tall or too short or too blonde or not blonde enough," she said. "You have to learn not to take it personally, and it isn't easy."

Then Jessi told Claire about callbacks and agents and meetings and endless rehearsals. She told her about the time she visited Derek Masters on the set of his TV show, and about how *boring* it can be on a TV or movie set — how it can take all day to film one little scene. And she told her about how entertainers have to perform all the time, even if they're sick, or tired, or injured. "That's what they mean when they say, 'the show must go on,' " Jessi explained.

"But — but isn't it fun when people clap after you do something good?" Claire asked. "Or when they laugh at a joke you tell? Or cry when you sing a sad song?"

"Sure," said Jessi. "That's why so many people stay in show business even though it's such hard work. For some people, those good things make all the bad things worthwhile."

"I never thought about the bad things," said Claire. "I just thought about having a dressing room with a big star on the door, and lots of fancy dresses, and a big long car to pick me up and drive me everywhere I want to go."

"Not too many people get all that," said Jessi with a grin.

Claire didn't grin back. Instead she said solemnly, "Jessi? I'm not so sure I want to be in show business anymore. I mean, I'd like to be a star, but not if it takes so much hard work."

Jessi nodded. "I can understand that," she said, reaching over to give Claire a little hug.

Suddenly, Claire broke away from Jessi and sat up straight. "Oh, no!" she cried. She put her hand over her mouth.

"What?" asked Jessi.

"My video!" said Claire. "I don't want that agent to see it. We have to get it back before she watches it!"

"I don't think we can," said Jessi. "It's already in the mail."

"Oh no!" Claire wailed. "What am I going to do?"

"Well," said Jessi. "I guess you just have to hope the agent doesn't like your tape." She

106

knew from experience that in show business rejection happens a lot more than acceptance.

Claire nodded. "But what if she *does* like it?" she asked miserably.

Jessi smiled. A few minutes ago Claire was dying to be discovered. "If she likes it, and she wants to make you a star, I guess you'll just have to tell her you changed your mind," said Jessi.

"That would be so, so embarrassing," replied Claire. Just the thought of it seemed to make her blush. "But I guess that's what I'll have to do." She stood up. "I don't think I want to talk about this anymore," she said. "Can I go out and play with Margo?"

"Of course," said Jessi. She gave Claire another hug, hoping to see her smile. But Claire hugged her back listlessly and walked slowly outside. Jessi felt awful. But she realized this was probably for the best. After all, it was better for Claire to find out ahead of time how hard show business could be.

Jessi followed Claire outside and watched with Mal as Claire and Margo played hopscotch.

"What happened?" whispered Mal. "Claire looks so sad."

Jessi told her about their conversation.

"That's too bad," said Mal. "But she'll cheer up soon. And I have to say that my whole family will thank you. Maybe we won't have to watch that video anymore!"

The girls giggled. Just then, they heard a horn honk, and saw Mrs. Arnold leaning out of her car window. She had pulled up in front of the Pikes' house. "Hello, girls," she said. "The twins and I are off to the museum. They've been after me to take them back there ever since the first time they went. They just loved the Discovery Room. Anyway, we were wondering if anybody would like to come along."

"Me!" cried Claire, looking more cheerful already.

"Me, too," said Margo. "Can we, Mallory?"

"Sure," said Mal. "I bet Vanessa would like to go, too."

"I'll go get her," said Claire. She ran into the house.

Mal and Jessi decided that Mal would stay home with the boys, who were busy with their treehouse, while Jessi went along with the girls.

"Can we all squeeze into your car?" Jessi asked Mrs. Arnold.

"Sure," said Mrs. Arnold, with a grin. "The more, the merrier."

Soon they were on their way. Jessi told me later that she had to smile when she heard Claire leading the other girls in a few rounds of "Row, row, row your boat." She was glad Claire still liked to sing, even if she didn't want to do it professionally anymore.

The museum was full that afternoon. Every room was packed with loud, happy kids. "It made the museum seem so alive," said Jessi later.

Jessi and Mrs. Arnold let the girls decide where to go and what activities to do. They followed them from room to room and watched as the girls discovered exhibits they hadn't seen yet.

After awhile, Jessi asked Mrs. Arnold if she could sneak off to check out the Don Newman exhibit, since she had heard so much about it from me. Mrs. Arnold said she'd be glad to watch all the girls for a few minutes, so Jessi found her way to the sculpture gallery.

She loved the show, she told me later. But the most important thing about her visit to the Newman exhibit was what she found out when she started talking to one of the guards there. She told him how much she liked the PLEASE TOUCH signs, and that Don Newman must be a very cool guy. The guard agreed. He was excited because the entire museum staff had been invited to Friday's party. "Not many artists would have thought of inviting the staff, but Newman did," he said.

"What about security, if you'll all be at the party?" Jessi asked.

"Oh, they're not so worried about that anymore," said the guard. "Security has been really tight for a week, and nothing has happened, so they're loosening up a little. Say, you're not planning a robbery, are you?" He grinned at Jessi.

"No way," she said, grinning in return. Then she headed back to the kids' area to find Mrs. Arnold and the girls. By the end of their afternoon at the museum, Claire seemed to be feeling a lot better. In fact, she seemed to have decided on a new career. At least, that was what Jessi thought when Claire asked her seriously, "Do scientists have to audition?"

CHAPTER 13

"So anyway, it sounds like security isn't going to be so tight anymore," said Jessi. It was Friday afternoon, and my friends and I were gathered in my room for our BSC meeting. Jessi was telling us what she'd learned at the museum the day before. "The guard I talked to was really nice," she added.

"Most of the people who work at the museum seem nice," mused Kristy.

"Except for Mr. Snipes," I muttered. "He's a big creep. And maybe a thief, too."

"Maybe," said Mal. "But not definitely."

"I know," I said. "I'm planning to keep an eye on him when I'm at the party tonight, but I plan to watch *everybody* closely. The thief could be any one of the museum's employees. The guards, the maintenance crew, the salespeople in the shop. As far as I'm concerned, everybody's a suspect. I still think the thief is

Mr. Snipes, but until I'm positive I'm not counting *anyone* out."

"Good thinking," said Kristy approvingly. "While we're waiting for calls, why don't we go over the facts of the case one more time? Maybe we'll think of something new, the way you did the other day."

"All right," I said. "Well, let's see. First of all, the coins were stolen last Thursday."

"Can you believe it's only been a little over a week since that happened?" interrupted Stacey. "It feels like years. Sorry, Claud. Go on."

"Okay," I said. "On Friday, the newspaper had an article about the robbery. On Saturday, five of us went to the museum to do some investigating, but we didn't find out much until later in the day when I noticed that the Newman sculpture felt funny. Then Stacey and I met Mr. Snipes and decided something was strange about him. I snagged his resume. On Sunday, we went to the library and found out about robberies that took place at other museums he's worked at. On Wednesday, I figured out that the coins must have been stolen by an insider — somebody who works at the museum."

"Brilliant deductive reasoning, Miss Nancy Drew of Stoneybrook," Kristy spoke up, with a grin.

I smiled. "Wednesday was also the day I called Don Newman and he invited me to the party. And on Thursday, Jessi found out that the museum is planning to cut down on security." I took a deep breath. "Is that everything?"

Everyone nodded.

"I have to say," said Mal, "that Mr. Snipes looks awfully suspicious. There have been robberies at other museums where he's worked, he definitely qualifies as an insider, and he seems like a creepy guy."

"I know," I replied. "But what about the man with one blue eye and one green eye? Let's not forget about him. He was at the museum the day of the robbery, and at the museum again when we went back the next day."

"But does he work for the museum?" asked Jessi. "Would he have had a key to that case?"

"Who knows?" I said, shrugging.

"That Brownie troop you told us about was there, too," said Mary Anne with a giggle. "Are they still suspects?"

We all cracked up. "I haven't heard any reports of ancient coins being used to buy Gummi worms at the candy store," said Stacey.

At that point, the phone began ringing with parents calling to arrange jobs. We were pretty busy for awhile, and we were surprised when Kristy pointed to the clock. "Meeting's over," she said. It was six o'clock.

"Oh, my lord!" I said. "I'm supposed to be at that party in three hours. Forget about the mystery! This will be my first formal party, I'm going to meet a famous artist — and I have no idea what to wear!"

"You look nice in what you have on now," said Kristy. "Why don't you just wear that?"

I looked down at myself. I was wearing a pair of bright red leggings topped by a white man-tailored shirt and a vest that used to belong to my father. Only Kristy would think my outfit qualified as "formal." I shook my head and smiled at her. "I don't think so," I said. I jumped up to look into my closet for the millionth time in two days. "You guys have to help me," I said. "This is an emergency!"

Unfortunately, Kristy, Jessi, Mal, and Shannon had to leave, emergency or not. But Mary Anne and Stacey agreed to stay and help me.

"Have fun," said Kristy as she left with the others. "Don't be nervous. I know you'll have a blast."

So far, I hadn't been too nervous. But suddenly, I began to feel flustered. What if I couldn't find anything decent to wear? What if I made a fool of myself in front of Don Newman? How would I know how to act at such a fancy party? Mary Anne must have seen the look on my face.

"It'll be fine," she said soothingly. "We'll get you all set."

The three of us agreed that we should eat something first, so we trooped downstairs and raided the kitchen. (My parents were at a meeting, and Janine was working away on her computer.)

Stacey made herself a cheese sandwich. Mary Anne heated up a can of soup and found some crackers. But I didn't feel hungry at all. "I wouldn't even be tempted by a bag of Cheez Doodles," I said. "Not that I would ever find a thing like that in *this* kitchen."

Mary Anne made me eat a small bowl of chicken noodle soup and two crackers. "If you don't eat, you might pass out from hunger in the middle of the party," she said. That image was enough to make me drain my bowl to the last noodle.

After we ate, we headed back upstairs. "All right," said Stacey. "Now, what kind of look were you thinking of?" She threw open my closet door and stood staring at my clothes. "Sophisticated? Arty? Trendy?"

"I don't know," I said miserably. "A combination of all those things would be good, I guess. I mean, I want to look like *myself*, only more dressed up, you know?"

Stacey pulled out a black velvet dress. "How about this?" she asked.

I shook my head. "Boring," I said.

She nodded and threw it on the bed. "What about these silk pants?"

"Are pants okay at a formal party?" asked Mary Anne doubtfully. "You don't want to look like a kid who doesn't know how to dress."

"Ditch the pants," I said immediately.

Stacey pulled outfit after outfit out of my closet. I have a *lot* of clothes, but nothing seemed right. Most of them are fine for school, or even for special events like dances or parties. But nothing looked right for a party like this one. A *grown-up* party.

"You look terrific in this," Stacey said, holding up a bright blue sweater-dress.

"Thanks," I said. "But it's not right, either."

"Do you think I could borrow it?" she asked.

"Sure," I said, falling back onto my bed. "Oh, this is a disaster," I moaned. "We'll never find anything." Mary Anne patted my arm sympathetically.

"What's this?" Stacey asked, reaching into the back of the closet and coming out with a long, silky pale green robe embroidered in gorgeous colors.

116

I stared at it. "That's — that's one of Mimi's kimonos," I said. My grandmother wore regular clothes most of the time, but she had brought some beautiful kimonos with her when she came to this country from Japan as a girl. She wore them for special family occasions sometimes, and she always looked graceful and young when she did. Seeing the kimono made me miss Mimi terribly.

"This is it!" said Stacey.

"What?" I asked.

"This is what you'll wear tonight. Put it on." She handed it to me. "I just have a feeling this will be perfect."

I took off my vest and shirt, and slipped on the kimono. The silk felt soft and light against my skin. It seemed to float around me. I tied the sash (which Mimi called an "obi") around my waist and stood up straight.

"Wow," said Mary Anne softly.

"Awesome," said Stacey. "You look totally awesome."

I walked to the mirror to see for myself. The green and blue colors of the kimono set off my black hair, and the long, fluttering sleeves looked romantic. For half a second, I saw Mimi's face instead of mine in the mirror, and I felt tears come to my eyes. It was almost as if she were in the room with me, urging me to wear the kimono to the party. "I'll wear it," I said. "Definitely." I smiled at the mirror.

"Let's put your hair up and find some accessories that will go with the outfit," Stacey said. She started to rummage through my jewelry box. "These earrings will be perfect."

"You look wonderful," said Mary Anne. I thought I saw tears gleaming in her eyes, too. She had been very close to Mimi, and I know she misses her almost as much as I do.

I pulled my hair into a modified French twist, put on the earrings, and added a few gold bracelets. Then I put on my makeup. "Hand me that lip gloss, will you, Stace?" I said. She and Mary Anne stood behind me, watching. "Now all I have to do is figure out how to act at this party. I mean, it's not going to be like a school dance, where the boys stand around on one side and crack jokes and the girls stand around on the other side and giggle. This is an adult party, and I'll have to act like an adult."

"It's true," said Stacey. "You wouldn't want to pull any tricks like bringing a rubber tarantula to tease people with." One of Stacey's dates did that once, at a dance. Can you believe it?

"Okay," said Mary Anne. "Time for the etiquette quiz. First of all, what do you say when you meet Don Newman?"

"Um, I guess I say 'Hi, Don,' " I answered. "He said to call him that."

"No way," said Mary Anne. "This is a fancy party. You have to call him Mr. Newman, at least at first."

"Okay," I said. "What else?"

"Watch out when you go to the ladies room. Be careful not to get toilet paper stuck to the bottom of your shoe and drag it back out to the party with you," advised Stacey.

We cracked up, but I blushed at the thought.

"Don't drink anything that might stain the kimono if you spill it," said Mary Anne. "And don't eat anything that might get stuck in your teeth."

Mary Anne had a whole storehouse of etiquette tips, from how to shake hands to how to make small talk with strangers. Stacey added a few of her own, and soon I felt ready for anything. I was still feeling nervous, though. "Thanks, guys," I said as I saw them out the door. "I couldn't have done it without you."

"No problem," said Stacey. "You look gorgeous."

"I have one more tip for you," said Mary Anne, with a smile. She leaned close to me and spoke very seriously. "Just remember this. Have a *great* time!"

CHAPTER 14

I tightened the sash around my waist one more time as my father and I stepped out of the car. He looked handsome in his dark suit and tie. He smiled at me. "Ready, my dear?" he said, crooking his arm so I could put mine through it.

I took a deep breath. "Ready," I said. I was feeling as nervous as a cat in a room full of dogs. But we walked up the stairs and through the main door of the museum, and within seconds I had forgotten about being nervous. "Awesome," I whispered, looking around. The main lobby was full of men and women, and every one of them was dressed to the teeth. Some of the men were even wearing tuxedos. A lot of the women were wearing floor-length gowns, and I saw plenty of expensive-looking jewelry. I glanced down at my kimono and smiled. I knew I had made the right choice. I felt comfortable, but I looked dressed up and exotic.

"Everyone seems to be heading toward the Egypt Room," said my dad. "Shall we?" He offered his arm again. We stopped outside the room to pick up name tags from a table, and then walked into the party.

I hadn't been in the Egypt Room before, since I had spent most of my time in the rooms meant for children and in the gallery. But as soon as I saw it, I knew it would become one of my favorite parts of the museum. I saw mummy cases with painted faces and fascinating symbols drawn on them. And I saw glass cases full of ancient jewelry. Hieroglyphics were painted on the walls, and there were panels with those pictures of people who seem to be walking sideways.

I wanted to look at everything, but the room was so full it was hard to see the displays. Everyone was talking and laughing and eating pastries and drinking champagne. Waiters dressed in starched white shirts and black pants circulated among the guests, passing silver trays. I took a cracker spread with what looked like cheese from one tray, and a glass of cider from another, and then I just stood back and watched the crowd. Everyone was wearing name tags, and I had this feeling all of a sudden that I was in the middle of a scene in a murder mystery, the part where the whole cast of characters is assembled and the culprit is about to be revealed.

I looked around to see if I recognized anyone. It didn't take long to find someone. There, next to a woman in a blue-sequined dress, was the man with one blue eye and one green eye. I felt a shiver run up my spine. He seemed to be looking around the room, as if he, too, were checking out the crowd. He wore a fancy black suit with a shiny stripe down the side of his trouser legs.

Unlike me, my dad seemed relaxed. He stood next to me, eating crackers and drinking club soda. "Do you see Don Newman?" he asked.

"I think that's him over by the small mummy case," I said, trying to sound calm. "I recognize him from his picture in the paper." At the moment, he was surrounded by people, so it didn't seem like the right time to introduce myself. Dad and I stood there for awhile. I was trying to keep tabs on the man with the funny eyes, and I was also watching out for any other suspects. Then I noticed that Don Newman was walking toward a jewelry case, and I could see that he was alone. I pulled my father's sleeve. "Come on," I said. We walked quickly across the room. "Excuse me," I said. He turned, and I checked his name tag just to make sure it was him. "Mr. Newman, I'm Claudia Kishi," I said, remembering what Mary Anne had told me. I felt a little nervous again, but not much. Mr. Newman looked as friendly in person as he sounded over the phone.

"Claudia," he said, shaking my hand. "Please, call me Don. It's a pleasure to meet you. What a lovely kimono you're wearing."

"Thanks," I said. "This is my father, John Kishi." "Dad, this is Don Newman." They shook hands.

"Nice party," said my father. The three of us stood chatting for a few minutes, about the museum and how nice it was for Stoneybrook to have it. Then my dad looked at me. "Claudia, I just spotted some friends. Mind if I go talk to them?"

"Okay," I replied. Actually, I was glad to see him go, so that Mr. Newman — Don — and I could talk about the mystery.

My dad said good-bye to us, and wandered off. "So, Claudia," said Don, turning to me. "Are you enjoying the party?"

I hesitated. "Well, it's very nice," I said. "But I can't stop thinking about your sculpture, and how different it felt. I'm just so sure there's something funny going on here." At that moment, I saw Mr. Snipes walk by. "And I think *he* may have something to do with it," I whispered.

"The curator?" asked Don. "But — "

"I can't explain right now," I whispered. I was watching Mr. Snipes mingle with the guests. Then I noticed that he was about to leave the room. Without thinking, I grabbed Don's sleeve. "Come on!" I said. "Let's follow him."

Don grinned. "This is exciting," he said. "Much more fun than a boring old party." He followed me, and I followed Mr. Snipes out the door, back into the main lobby, and down a dimly lit hall. Guess where we followed him to? His office door.

"Oops," I said, turning to Don. I knew I was blushing. I had led us to a dead end.

"That's okay," he said. "Listen, as long as we've left the party, how would you like to check out the sculpture?"

"I'd love to," I said. We walked to the sculpture gallery, but when we reached it, the door was locked.

"That's strange," said Don. He led me back down the hall and we found a guard, one of the few on duty that night. "I'm Don Newman," he said. "Do you know why the sculpture gallery is locked?"

"The show has been taken down already,"

said the guard. "All of your sculptures are in storage room B, ready to be packed up for shipment to your next show."

Don nodded. "I see," he said. "Thank you."

We walked away from the guard. "Well, I guess that's that," said Don.

"Let's check out the storage room," I said. I couldn't stand the thought of giving up.

Don looked at me, his eyes twinkling. "You're very tenacious," he said. "Okay, why not?"

I didn't know what "tenacious" meant until I looked it up later. So I didn't know whether Don was complimenting me or insulting me. He didn't *look* as if he were insulting me, so I just smiled. (I found out later that "tenacious" means, basically, *stubborn*. I guess it was kind of a compliment, under the circumstances.)

We found storage room B near the gift shop, down a darkened hall. "It'll probably be locked," said Don as we approached the door.

I was reaching for the knob when I heard footsteps. "Shh!" I said. I grabbed Don's arm and pulled him into a dark corner. We watched as a custodian, pushing a mop and bucket, walked to the door of the storage room. He was wearing a Walkman, and he hummed to himself as he pulled out a large ring filled with keys, rummaged through them, and then stuck one into the keyhole and pushed the door open. He walked in and flipped on a light, and we tiptoed to the doorway and peered through.

The custodian pushed his bucket over to the sculpture called Daphne. My eyes widened and I exchanged looks with Don. We stepped inside, since the man's back was toward us. Then, as we watched, the custodian tipped the sculpture up, put his hand inside a hidden opening, and pulled something out. I nearly fainted when I saw what it was. Coins! A handful of shining, gold coins. I gasped.

Don put his finger to his lips. The custodian, who was still humming to himself, dropped the coins into his bucket — and turned around. When he saw us, his face turned white. "I — I — " He started to say something, but seemed to change his mind. Instead of talking, he shoved his bucket toward us and turned to run.

Don lunged at the custodian and tackled him. From behind me, I heard running footsteps, and before I knew what was happening, a third man barreled into the room and jumped on top of Don. I stood still, unable to move or scream, staring at the pile of arms and legs. Suddenly I realized who had tackled Don. I saw a black stripe running up a trouser leg. It was the man with one blue eye and one green eye!

CHAPTER 15

Dear Dawn,,
    You won't believe
what has been happening
here. California may
be exciting, but it's
nothing compared to
Stoneybrook. Claudia
just solved a huge
mystery. See, some coins
were stolen from the
new museum, and then
there was this sculpture
that felt funny to
Claud, and then she
and the guy who made
the sculpture, caught
the thief! I know, I
know, it all sounds
really complicated. Maybe
I should let Kristy try
to explain.   Love you!

It's not all that complicated. It's really simple, actually. The guy with one blue eye and one green eye turned out to be a private eye, and the curator's not such a bad guy after all.

Wait a minute, wait a minute. Dawn doesn't even know anything about the guy with the different - colored eyes. See, we thought he might be a suspect, because he was there when the robbery took place. And one day we followed him all over the museum until he finally got into his car and drove off. Then it turns out he was on our side, really. When we talked to him after the press conference, he told us we were making him crazy that day, and that driving off was the only way he could think of to lose us! Everyone laughed.

I bet you're surprised to hear there was a press conference. Well there was, and will send you a copy of the Stoneybrook News to prove it.

Mr. Snipes shook Claud's hand and made her an "honorary trustee" of the museum.

Dawn, you must be totally confused by now! We're not explaining ourselves very well. Okay, let me try. See, Mr. Snipes is the curator of the museum, and for a long time we thought he might be the thief, because he acted kind of creepy and there had been robberies at other museums he worked at. But we found out that preventing robberies is his specialty, and he's often hired by museums who feel they are vulnerable to theft. What a surprise that was!

Dawn, you probably don't have any idea what happened. Basically, all you have to know is that the bad guy was caught and Claudia was responsible for his capture. We'll tell you the details another time. We miss you!

Dawn, I whish you culd have been here for this mistery. It was ahsome. But I dont' desserv all the creddit. Evryboddy helped out. The coolist part of the hole thing is that now that I'm a trusty of the museem, I get to go to all the opening nigth partys and bring as many freinds as I want. Come back soon so you can come two!

Love, Claudia Nancy Drew Kishi

Dawn was sure to be confused by that letter, but I knew it would seem clearer after she read the newspaper article we had enclosed. Plus, Mary Anne could set her straight the next time they talked on the phone. Curators, men with different-colored eyes, sculptures that moved — the mystery did seem complicated. But really, it was very simple.

I better explain what happened after that pile-up in storage room B. I was still rooted to the floor. Don was holding down the custodian, who was struggling to get to his feet. And the man with one green eye and one blue eye was on the top of the heap, yelling, "Nobody move! I'm a federal officer!"

Within moments, Mr. Snipes appeared in the room. He had heard the commotion and called the police, who arrived soon after. Then, once the men on the floor had untangled themselves, we began to sort things out.

The man with the funny eyes turned out to be named Mr. Olinger. He was a federal agent who specialized in art theft. He had been assigned to the Stoneybrook Museum when Mr. Snipes had been appointed curator. I guess the trustees of the museum had been warned that the museum was vulnerable to theft, and they thought the team of Olinger and Snipes could solve the problem.

The trustees didn't count on Mr. Will Saries, though. That was the custodian's name. Only he wasn't really a custodian. He was a thief who had been planning this robbery since before the museum opened. His plan was basically a good one, too. First, he set off the fire alarm as a distraction. Then, he *did*, as I had guessed, steal the coins by using his key to open the case. After that, he broke the case to cover up the evidence, which set off the burglar alarm. In the confusion that followed, he dumped the coins into his bucket. Later, he stashed them in Don's sculpture. (He knew about the special hiding place because he had helped to unpack Daphne when they were first setting up the exhibit.) His only problem came when, after the robbery, the museum tightened security and posted guards twenty-four hours a day. He didn't get a chance to retrieve the coins until the night of the party, when the security was relaxed.

He had made arrangements to sell the coins to a museum in Switzerland, and he was hoping to retire on the money he would make. Now, as Kristy said, "It looks like he'll be retiring behind bars."

I got all kinds of attention for helping to catch the robber. Actually, I thought it was mostly luck, but I had to admit that I would never have been in that room if I hadn't been trying to figure out the case.

"Teen Detective Helps Nab Coin Thief," read the headline in the *Stoneybrook News*. In the story was a funny quote from my father, who said he had no idea that his daughter was "an ace detective." And below the headline was a big picture of me, Don Newman, Mr. Snipes, and Mr. Olinger. Mr. Snipes was shaking my hand and grinning.

I never told Mr. Snipes that my friends and I had suspected him. I was too embarrassed. He turned out to be a pretty nice guy after all. I think he was just really busy and preoccupied when I first met him. And guess what? My fantasy came true, sort of. Now that I'm an honorary trustee, Mr. Snipes wants me to help him set up a show of local student work. "Including your own, of course," he said. I can't wait.

On Friday, a week after the mystery was solved, my friends and I celebrated by ordering in a pizza after our club meeting. While we ate it, we passed around the letter that we were writing to Dawn. Kristy read aloud from the newspaper article, to entertain us. "Ms. Kishi, a student at Stoneybrook Middle School, says she has no formal training in detective work. Yet federal agent Olinger insists that her follow-up on clues was 'professional and complete. She's tenacious,' said Olinger. 'She'd make a wonderful agent someday.' "

Tenacious. There was that word again. I told my friends what it meant, and they agreed that I can be extremely tenacious. "You're tenacious about not giving up your Nancy Drew books," Mallory pointed out.

"Or your junk food," added Stacey.

"And you're definitely tenacious about not doing your homework on time," said Kristy, giggling.

I laughed and blushed at the same time. "Well, you guys are pretty tenacious, too," I said. "I couldn't have solved this mystery without your help. How about a pizza toast?"

We picked up our pizza slices and bumped them together, as if they were champagne glasses. "Here's to Claud!" said Stacey. "The best detective in Stoneybrook." Pizza toasts may be silly, but they're one of my favorite BSC traditions.

Jessi was looking at the newspaper again. "This is a great picture of you, Claud," she said. "You should cut it out and frame it."

"I just might," I said. "My parents like that picture, too. They must have bought a dozen copies of the paper so they could send it to our friends and relatives."

Look for Mystery #12

DAWN AND THE SURFER GHOST

I huddled in my blanket and smiled over at Sunny, who was wrapped up, too. We both love ghost stories, and this seemed like the perfect setting. Of course, the stories that the kids were telling were fairly tame, not like some I know.

My thoughts were interrupted by a cry from Erick. "Look at that!" he said, pointing out toward the ocean. I turned to look, and I caught a glimpse of a faraway movement, though it was hard to make out much through the mist.

Within seconds, everybody was on their feet. (Everybody except the little kids, who were asleep, of course.) We stared out at the breakers, trying to figure out what it was we were seeing.

About the Author

ANN M. MARTIN did *a lot* of baby-sitting when she was growing up in Princeton, New Jersey. She is a former editor of books for children, and was graduated from Smith College.

Ms. Martin lives in New York City with her cats, Mouse and Rosie. She likes ice cream and *I Love Lucy*; and she hates to cook.

Ann Martin's Apple Paperbacks include *Yours Turly, Shirley; Ten Kids, No Pets; With You and Without You; Bummer Summer*; and all the other books in the Baby-sitters Club series.

"You're a star," said Stacey. "No doubt about it."

"Speaking of stars," I said, "I've been so busy with the mystery that I almost forgot about Claire. What's happening with her video?"

Mallory laughed. "Well, the agent sent it back," she said. "She said Claire has a lot of promise, but that she isn't looking for her 'type' at the moment."

"What's Claire's 'type'?" asked Stacey. "Silly brown-haired five-year-olds with blue eyes?"

Mal laughed again. "That must be it," she said. "Anyway, the agent was really nice to write a note like that. I think it made Claire feel better about being rejected."

"I thought she *wanted* to be rejected!" said Jessi. "At least, that's what she said the last time I saw her."

"Well, she did, in a way," said Mal. "I mean, I don't think she was ready for true stardom. But being turned down never feels good."

We nodded. That made sense. "She must be relieved, though," said Mary Anne.

"Not really," replied Mallory. "She still can't believe the agent didn't accept her. But you haven't heard the funniest part yet."

"What's that?" I asked.

"It turns out that Claire's kindergarten class is planning to put on a production of Hansel and Gretel. They all tried out for parts, and guess who got the role of the witch? Claire!"

"So she's on her way to a career on the stage anyway," I said, laughing. "That's great!"

My friends and I talked and ate pizza for a while longer, and then the party broke up. After everyone had left, I cleared the pizza box off my desk and pulled a sketch pad out from under my bed. I added the finishing touches to a drawing I had been working on all week, and then I rolled it up and stuck it into a mailing tube. I addressed the package to Don Newman. It was a drawing of the sculpture called Daphne, and with it I had enclosed a note.

I thot you'd like to have this. I hope you will allways remember me as one of your biggest fans and as your parntner in solving Stonybrok's famouse museum robery.
Sinserly yours,
Claudia Kishi

"It's a surfer," breathed Sunny, who was standing next to me.

"But why would anybody be surfing on this kind of night?" wondered Alyssa.

Alyssa was right. It was hardly an ideal night for surfing, with all that mist. And even with the moon shining, it was pretty dark.

I looked again, but I couldn't see anything this time. Erick began to run, leading a group of kids along the beach toward the last place we had seen the figure. Sunny and I followed after them. By the time we arrived at the edge of the water, there was nothing to be seen out on the ocean.

"A ghost!" said Erick. "It was a ghost, I bet you anything."

"A surfer ghost?" said Sunny.

"I bet it's the ghost of Thrash," I said quietly. I was hugging myself, trying to stay warm. Suddenly, I couldn't stop shivering.

#10 *Sea City, Here We Come!*
The Baby-sitters head back to the Jersey shore for some fun in the sun!

Mysteries:

1 *Stacey and the Missing Ring*
Stacey's being accused of taking a valuable ring. Can the Baby-sitters help clear her name?

2 *Beware, Dawn!*
Someone is playing pranks on Dawn when she's baby-sitting — and they're *not* funny.

3 *Mallory and the Ghost Cat*
It looks and sounds like a cat — but is it real?

4 *Kristy and the Missing Child*
Kristy organizes a search party to help the police find a missing child.

5 *Mary Anne and the Secret in the Attic*
Mary Anne discovers a secret about her past and now she's afraid of the future!

6 *The Mystery at Claudia's House*
Claudia's room has been ransacked! Can the Baby-sitters track down whodunnit?

7 *Dawn and the Disappearing Dogs*
Someone's been stealing dogs all over Stoneybrook!

8 *Jessi and the Jewel Thieves*
Jessi and her friend Quint are busy tailing two jewel thieves from the Big Apple!

9 *Kristy and the Haunted Mansion*
Kristy and the Krashers are spending the night in a spooky old house!

Don't miss out on
The All New

BABY·SITTERS®

Fan Club

Join now!
Your one-year membership package includes:

- The exclusive Fan Club T-Shirt!
- A Baby-sitters Club poster!
- A Baby-sitters Club note pad and pencil!
- An official membership card!
- The exclusive *Guide to Stoneybrook!*

Plus four additional newsletters per year

so you can be the first to know the hot news about the series — Super Specials, Mysteries, Videos, and more — the baby-sitters, Ann Martin, and lots of baby-sitting fun from the Baby-sitters Club Headquarters!

ALL THIS FOR JUST $6.95 plus $1.00 postage and handling! **You can't get all this great stuff anywhere else except THE BABY-SITTERS FAN CLUB!**

Just fill in the coupon below and mail with payment to: THE BABY-SITTERS FAN CLUB, Scholastic Inc., P.O. Box 7500, 2931 E. McCarty Street, Jefferson City, MO 65102.

THE BABY-SITTERS FAN CLUB

___ YES! Enroll me in The Baby-sitters Fan Club! I've enclosed my check or money order (no cash please) for $7.95

Name _____ Birthdate _____

Street _____

City _____ State/Zip _____

Where did you buy this book?

❏ Bookstore   ❏ Drugstore   ❏ Supermarket
❏ Book Fair   ❏ Book Club   ❏ other_____

BSFC593

Create Your Own
Mystery Stories!

THE BABY-SITTERS CLUB®

MYSTERY GAME!

WHO: Boyfriend   **WHY:** Romance

WHAT: Phone Call   **WHERE:** Dance

Use the special Mystery Case card to pick WHO did it, WHAT was involved, WHY it happened and WHERE it happened. Then dial secret words on your Mystery Wheels to add to the story! Travel around the special Stoneybrook map gameboard to uncover your friends' secret word clues! Finish four baby-sitting jobs and find out all the words to win. Then have everyone join in to tell the story!

Create Your Own Mystery Story as You Uncover the Clues!

YOU'LL FIND THIS
GREAT MILTON BRADLEY GAME
AT TOY STORES AND BOOKSTORES
NEAR YOU!

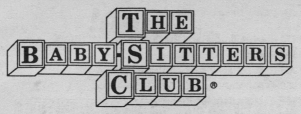

THE BABY-SITTERS CLUB®

by Ann M. Martin

More titles... ▶

The Baby-sitters Club titles continued...

Available wherever you buy books...or use this order form.

Scholastic Inc., P.O. Box 7502, 2931 E. McCarty Street, Jefferson City, MO 65102

Please send me the books I have checked above. I am enclosing $——————
(please add $2.00 to cover shipping and handling). Send check or money order - no
cash or C.O.D.s please.

Name ———————————————————————————————————

Address ———————————————————————————————————

City———————————————— State/Zip ————————————— .

Please allow four to six weeks for delivery. Offer good in the U.S. only. Sorry, mail orders are not
available to residents of Canada. Prices subject to change.